After Maya had gone, Blaise sniffed the faint trail of stirringly sensual perfume that his entrancing temporary visitor had left in her wake, and a charge of electricity zigzagged powerfully through the taut mid-section of his stomach.

It wasn't just the arresting notes of amber and warm tangerine that had stirred his previously slumbering libido. It was the intoxicating sight of almond-shaped green eyes fringed with sooty black lashes, long dark hair as glossy and as glittering as a moonlit sea, and audacious curves poured into the most seductive black velvet dress he'd ever seen.

With a brief shake of his head and a rueful smile, he went back to the comfortable winged armchair and the decanter of port his host had so thoughtfully provided, wondering when had been the last time a woman had so easily and carelessly refused him anything. His mind instantly provided him with the disturbing answer…*never.*

SECRETARY BY DAY, MISTRESS BY NIGHT

BY
MAGGIE COX

First published in Great Britain 2010
Harlequin Mills & Boon Limited,
Eton House, 18-24 Paradise Road, Richmond, Surrey TW9 1SR

© Maggie Cox 2010

ISBN: 978 0 263 21341 6

Harlequin Mills & Boon policy is to use papers that are natural, renewable and recyclable products and made from wood grown in sustainable forests. The logging and manufacturing process conform to the legal environmental regulations of the country of origin.

Printed and bound in Great Britain
by CPI Antony Rowe, Chippenham, Wiltshire

SECRETARY
BY DAY,
MISTRESS
BY NIGHT

To dear Danika—
my delightful companion on a wonderful creative
break in Northumberland—with love and thanks

CHAPTER ONE

Now she knew what E.T. must have felt like—alone and abandoned, light years away from what was loved and familiar, on a planet that seemed totally alien and unwelcoming. No wonder he'd sought refuge in Elliott's garage. Right now, Maya wished she could find a handy empty or darkened room to hide away in. One glance along the burnished candle-lit table at the high-octane guests, the reek of class and money, merely confirmed what she already knew to be true—she didn't fit in. A 'fish out of water,' that was what she was. But the truth was she didn't *want* to fit in.

Up until now her temporary jobs as an admin assistant had been pretty problem-free. But for the past few weeks her agency had asked her to work for a PR agency—Maya's *worst* nightmare as far as employment went. As the cut-glass accents rose and fell all around her, the scent of social snobbery in the air as distinct as Chanel No. 5, she knew *why* she resisted being part of such a phoney world.

She'd been raised by a father who'd all but sold his soul to perpetuate a similar lavish lifestyle and glean the dubious respect of such people, and in pursuit of it he had sacrificed everything that had once meant something to him. His talent, money, self-respect and once good reputation had been squandered and degraded as he lost his grip on reality and the values he'd once so fiercely upheld. And as he'd sunk lower and lower into a pit of self-loathing and regret for what he'd done, it had only been a matter of time before he took the ultimate terrible step.

Maya shuddered.

The devastating memory killed her appetite. Now the food on her plate held little temptation for her, and even knowing it had been specially created in a Michelin-starred restaurant for the purpose of the occasion was no incentive. Along with the dinner had come the services of one of the restaurant's top chefs, supported by a small team of staff to supervise its plating and serving. As was his usual style, her flamboyant boss, Jonathan Faraday, had spared no expense in displaying the growing success of his well-known PR company.

Clamping down on the persistent little flutter in her belly that urged her to get the hell out of there while she still had her pride and dignity intact, Maya lifted her gaze determinedly to the urbane silver-haired man sitting opposite and gave him the brightest smile she could muster.

Bad move, Maya. His startled hazel gaze flashed an invitation in return, and with a sinking feeling she knew he thought she'd given him the green light at last.

Hell's bells! What was she supposed to do now? Because it paid well, she didn't want to lose her job, but neither did she want to sleep with her boss to keep it. If only his super-efficient, elegant PA Caroline hadn't been called to the hospital bed of her dying mother-in-law at the last minute Maya would be safe at home now, dressed in comfy sweater and leggings; settling herself down on her sofa in readiness to view the film she'd hired for the weekend, with a bowl of tortilla chips, some salsa dip and a glass of wine on hand to heighten the experience.

Instead, she'd squeezed herself into a black velvet gown that was at least half a size too small, with her breasts crammed into a bodice so tight that it gave her the cleavage of a pneumatic glamour model, while her generously applied mascara made her eyes smart because it was new and she was obviously allergic to it. And all this discomfort because Jonathan had insisted she attend the function at his house in Caroline's place. It didn't matter that Maya was just a lowly temporary assistant from the less glamorous echelons of the company—Jonathan had had his eye on her for some time. He could see she had talent, determination, he'd said, smiling—and he could see she was destined for better things… *He could see this was a good opportunity to get into her knickers…*

Sighing heavily, she absently pushed the artistically arranged concoction of cranberries and parma-ham round her plate with a fork. When the blatant caress of a shoeless foot stroked up and down her ankle Maya almost jumped out of her skin. Tucking her feet indignantly beneath her chair, feeling searing heat hotter than a blacksmith's smithy assail her cheeks, she stared across the table at her suave, supremely confident boss. Bad enough she'd had an inkling that she might have to fight him off if he had too much to drink. Jonathan could more or less be counted on to chase anything in a skirt when his rampaging testosterone had been even more boosted by alcohol, but Maya hadn't expected he would be quite so blatant about it from the off. And all he'd had so far was one glass of champagne as the guests had been welcomed into the drawing room. In the name of self-preservation she had deliberately kept an eye on his intake—so she was surprised and more than a little rattled that he seemed intent on staking a claim right away. *Damn it, she shouldn't even be here!*

'Excuse me.'

'Something wrong, Miss Hayward?' Jonathan swirled the ruby-red wine that a passing waiter had just poured into his glass, leaning nonchalantly back in his grand Regency-style chair to enjoy the view as his shapely young employee rose hastily to her feet.

'No. I'm fine.'

Why did he have to notice everything she did? Was she forced to announce to the entire table that she had a sudden pressing need to visit the Ladies' Room? Why couldn't he just talk to the stunning blonde sitting next to him? The woman had been batting her eyelashes at him practically since they'd sat down. But apparently in the bedroom department Jonathan Faraday didn't give women his own age the time of day—no matter how beautiful. He liked them young, so she'd heard on the grapevine. *Bad luck for Maya that she'd only just turned twenty-five...*

'I'll—I'll be back shortly.'

Escaping before he could delay her further—or, worse, find some nefarious reason to accompany her— Maya found herself hurrying down corridors, the echo of her heels hitting the parquet floor mocking her as she struggled to find her bearings. *Oh, why had she agreed to this farce?* Now she was stuck out here in the middle of nowhere, dependent on her lech of a boss for a lift home—and not until midday tomorrow, if what Caroline had said was true. Apparently Jonathan was in no hurry to get back to London until mid-afternoon at least. Maya's head swam a little. The glass of champagne she'd had had been a dangerous lapse in judgement. She should have insisted on orange juice or mineral water. If she was going to get out of this little escapade with her virtue intact it was essential she kept a clear head—so no more alcohol for her, even if Jonathan insisted.

Her green eyes flicked hopefully round. *She could have sworn there was a bathroom round here somewhere...* Pushing open twin cream doors with ornate gilded panels, she found herself in a long, high-ceilinged room, its panelling painted in tastefully calming hues of pink and cream. A welcoming fire blazed in the huge marble fireplace, tempting her to stay and re-establish some of her lost composure.

Gazing round, Maya was momentarily distracted by the elaborate array of expensive-looking art that adorned the walls, and the seductive glow of antique lamps turned down low that cleverly created the illusion that the large, elegant room was actually more intimately proportioned than it really was. Succumbing to necessity, she gave in to the luxury of breathing out completely. Her tight bodice almost cracked a rib, while her lush breasts appeared in dire peril of escaping their velvet confines any time soon.

What had possessed her to wear such an outrageous dress? Okay, Caroline had told her the dress code was black tie and evening wear, but surely she knew that, when she'd borrowed the garment from her smaller-built friend Sadie, she was courting trouble by wearing it? *Especially* when Jonathan Faraday was around!

* * *

'If Jonathan's the confectioner, then clearly you've got to be the candy.'

At the sound of an amused yet obviously mocking male voice, Maya spun round in shock, mortified that she'd been observed when she had stupidly imagined herself to be alone. Her hand flew self-consciously to her cleavage, her teeth worrying at her plump lower lip as she stared at the man who suddenly rose from the high-winged chair turned towards the fireplace. Why hadn't she noticed he was there straight away? A shiver of embarrassment and frustration sprinted up her spine. Staring transfixed at the imposing stranger, she felt his electrifying gaze welding her to a hypnotised standstill.

'And you are…?' *Not that she really wanted to know, when inside she was silently fuming at his impertinent assumption that she had somehow been invited purely for decoration.*

'I see you haven't done your homework, Miss…?'

Of all the arrogant…!

'I work for Mr Faraday.'

'Of course you do. You *work* for me too in that dress, if I may say so?'

Scorching embarrassment immobilised her. *Blast that stupid dress!* And blast her eye-catching curves, when life would have been so much easier if she'd simply been straight up and down and flat-chested.

'If that was meant as a compliment, then forgive me if I don't take it as one. It's not at all flattering to be viewed as some kind of decorative object…as if I don't possess even a modicum of intelligence! I've met people like you before, and I'm…' Maya paused to take a breath, before biting her tongue. 'Yes, well… I'd better not say any more. Time to go, I think.'

'What do you mean, you've met people like me before?'

'Never mind.'

'Oh, but I *do* mind. Explain yourself.'

It was too late to rescind her comment, and Maya sensed her shoulders drop with resignation and not a little annoyance. 'Enough to say I'm not part of the floor show or entertainment for the guests, however it might look. I didn't even want to be here in the first place!'

The stranger's well-cut lips parted in a puzzled smile. 'This is getting more and more interesting. Why didn't you want to be here, Miss…?'

'Hayward.'

It was difficult to say with any sense of accuracy what colour his eyes were in the muted glow of the lamps—it sufficed to register that they burned with a fierce, concentrated gleam across the distance between them, keeping Maya prisoner even though she desperately wanted to flee. Beneath the bold regard of that disturbing glance she shifted uncomfortably. *Was it her, or had the room suddenly acquired the temperature of some tropical oasis?*

'I'm only here because of work. All I meant was this

isn't my kind of scene and neither are the people. I apologise if I've offended you in any way with my frankness.'

'Apology accepted. I'm not offended at all. Just intrigued.'

'I'd still better go.'

'I wish you wouldn't.' The man walked towards her and a sharp spasm of recognition jolted through Maya's insides. *Blaise Walker*—movie actor turned lauded and brilliant playwright. No wonder he had made that dig about her not doing her homework. He was the guest of honour, no less! The guest that Jonathan had announced to the table a mere ten minutes ago as being unavoidably detained.

Now her face burned for another reason. She had just been bordering on rude to the man, and no doubt Jonathan would hear all about it. But what was Blaise doing, hiding out in here? Her growing unease deepened. One, because the man was even more devastatingly attractive in the flesh than in his photographs, and two, because she didn't really think her boss would like the idea of a mere admin assistant like her fraternising with such an important client—let alone verbally putting him in his place! She should make herself scarce…*now*.

'Well, I have to go. I'm expected back any time now.'

'Of course…it's no surprise that a woman like you would be missed if you were away too long.'

'Look…I didn't mean to disturb you in any way. I

was just trying to find the Ladies' Room, but I'm afraid I—I got lost.'

'This is a big house.'

Did he think she hadn't noticed? It was an extremely impressive one too—a real showpiece. The kind to which her father would have relished inviting his illustrious clientele—which had included rock stars, film actors and art sycophants, who had bought his paintings during his short but infamous career—for drinks and other 'recreational' refreshments. The minuscule square footage of her studio apartment would fit into it at least a hundred times over, she was sure.

Renewing her intention to make herself scarce, Maya moved back towards the still ajar twin doors.

'Anyway, like I said…I'm sorry for the intrusion.'

'An apology is hardly necessary when the pleasure was all mine. Perhaps when you've visited the Ladies' Room you might consider coming back for a while, to give us a chance to get properly acquainted?'

'No!'

She hadn't meant to sound quite so adamant, but any further explanation somehow got stuck in her throat. The way Blaise Walker was surveying her—disturbing eyes mocking in that haunting angular face of his, tarnished gold hair darkly glinting against the startling white of his shirt collar—Maya was finding it seriously difficult to think straight. She just prayed he wouldn't reveal her inadvertent intrusion and blunt opinions to Jonathan when they met up. Her boss might want to bed her, but he wouldn't take it lightly if his client intimated that she'd bothered him in any way. Her hand curved anxiously around the brass door handle.

'Sorry…' she muttered once more as she exited hurriedly into the hallway.

After she'd gone, Blaise sniffed the faint trail of stirringly sensual perfume that his entrancing temporary visitor had left in her wake and a charge of electricity zigzagged powerfully through his taut mid-section. It wasn't just the arresting notes of amber and warm tangerine that had stirred his previously slumbering libido. It was the intoxicating sight of almond-shaped green eyes fringed with sooty black lashes, long dark hair as glossy as a glittering moonlit sea, and audacious curves poured into the most seductive black velvet dress he'd ever seen.

With a brief shake of his head and a rueful smile, he went back to the comfortable winged armchair and the decanter of port his host had so thoughtfully provided, wondering when the last time was that a woman had so easily and carelessly refused him anything. His mind instantly provided him with the disturbing answer…*never*.

Blaise drank down the remainder of his drink with far less enjoyment than he'd anticipated and frowned. There was a certain lack of respect that manifested itself in him around anything that came to him too easily. That went for success *and* women. It was only natural that a beautiful, feisty female like his alluring visitor—a woman who was clearly not going to tumble into his bed at the click of his fingers—would inevitably arouse his interest. But, that said, despite Miss Hayward's indignant assertion that she wasn't 'part of the floor show', it was fairly obvious that she must belong to Jonathan. *She had to.* She hadn't even bothered to deny it.

Dropping the crystal stopper a little impatiently into the decanter, he carefully returned it to the small rosewood table beside the chair. Raking his fingers through his sleek golden hair, he briefly closed his eyes, wishing he hadn't allowed Jane, his agent, to convince him that he should capitalise on the current avid interest in his work from the theatre-going public and take advantage of some first-rate PR to promote his image.

All Blaise wanted to do was retreat to his remote house in the wilds of Northumberland, with nothing but the mournful soughing of the wind and the untamed beauty of the countryside for company, write to his heart's content and let the world go its own tedious way without him.

He'd briefly become acquainted with fame during his three-year stint as a film actor, and the maelstrom of public interest at the time, as well as the intrusion into his private life, had been a right royal pain! If there were actors who craved fame, with all its dubious rewards and lack of privacy, then he wasn't one of them. All he had been interested in was conveying the character he played to the audience with the utmost conviction and one hundred percent commitment. If he could do that then he wouldn't have short-changed the people who had come to see him.

He applied the same passionate approach to his writing. Hopefully, when this current circus of media attention was over, he could return to Hawk's Lair and pull up the drawbridge—for a little while at least. But, that said, it didn't stop him continuing to speculate about the gorgeous brunette who'd inadvertently wandered in on him, with all that creamy cleavage so tantalisingly on display and a temper that—did she but know it—made her even *more* provocative than she was already.

His creative mind was already speculating on how that pent-up passion might be expressed in bed. Even more, it made him fantasise about helping her out of that sexy little dress later on tonight if even so much as *half* a chance came his way…

They stopped outside her bedroom door, with Maya twisting her arm behind her back to clutch anxiously at the doorknob as she desperately sought an escape route out of her predicament. Her boss swayed in front of her, alcoholic fumes making her grimace. Jonathan's drinking was legendary, but he had surpassed his own reputation tonight. In fact, Maya was amazed that he was still standing, never mind trying to coerce her into bed. His chameleon-like hazel eyes—a little cloudy now from the effects of alcohol—dropped lasciviously to her cleavage. He put a hand out to the side of her, to help balance himself against the wall.

Ignoring her seriously startled expression as he loomed over her, he capitalised on the opportunity to move his body even closer, so that along with the fumes of alcohol her senses were assaulted by the overpowering smell of his French cologne.

'I thought the dinner went really well tonight, didn't you? But I'm really tired now, and I—' Maya moved suddenly and darted to the side of him, just in time to deflect an oncoming caress, her heart racing so fast she was almost dizzy.

Frustrated and cross, Jonathan swore. 'Screw the dinner! All I want to do right now is take you to bed. Think about it, darling. A girl like you deserves so much more than an admin assistant's pay to get by on. Be nice to me and I'll make it more than worth your while… You get my drift, don't you, sweetie?'

He raised a perfectly groomed silver eyebrow to drive home his clumsily executed innuendo, reminding Maya so much of a dastardly rogue in one of those old silent movies that she almost laughed out loud. All that was missing was the famous handlebar moustache and the scene would be complete.

'Yes, Jonathan. I *do* get your drift. But at the end of the day you're my boss, and I make it a rule never to complicate professional relationships by allowing them to become personal.' She sucked in a deep breath, trying not to let her voice falter. 'I'm one of your employees...albeit a *temporary* one. That said, I'm going to decline your invitation and say goodnight. In the cold light of day I'm sure you'll be glad I did.'

'What if I offered you a permanent position? Would that help you see things differently?'

'No.' Maya had no hesitation in making that clear. 'I'm afraid it wouldn't.'

'What a shame,' Jonathan sneered. 'And I thought you were such a bright girl too. Still...you're not getting off that easily.'

'What do you mean?' Her green eyes flashed her alarm.

'You're just playing hard to get, aren't you?'

Suddenly there was an expression on his face that put every impulse in Maya's body on red alert. *This is going to be trickier than I thought...* She panicked. Letting go of the doorknob, she raked her long hair away from her face, letting her hand splay protectively across her chest.

'I don't know what you're talking about. I'm only here tonight because my job required it.'

'Don't tell me you're that naïve?' Jonathan breathed, yanking her towards him. 'Common or garden assistants don't get invited to my house just to take dictation! I've been flirting with you for weeks now—don't pretend you didn't know what it was leading to.'

'I'm here because Caroline was called away at the last

minute. She told me you needed someone to stand in for her,' Maya protested, even as Jonathan shook his head.

'Caroline stayed away because I *ordered* her to stay away!' he growled. 'Seeing as you turned me down every time I asked you out, it was the only way I could think of to get you alone. Has the penny finally dropped, *Miss* Hayward?'

She twisted her face away as his mouth descended, pushing hard against his chest with both hands, in a split second seeing all her effort and hard work wasted as she denied Jonathan Faraday the prize he craved, knowing she would get nothing for her pains but her marching orders.

Oh, well. She'd just have to tell the agency to find her something else. It would be a cold day in hell before she succumbed to sexual coercion from a man just to keep her job—that was for sure!

'Come on, Maya—giving me the runaround is one thing, but I've been working myself up to fever-pitch knowing you were coming to my house this weekend. Just one little kiss, eh?'

He might have been drunk, but Jonathan was physically no push-over. He easily hijacked her arms to pin her against the wall, breathing heavily as he pressed his body hard against hers, seeing the sudden fear darkening her lovely green eyes and no doubt getting off on the thought of having his way.

That was until an authoritative male voice a few feet

away said coolly, 'I must say I'm surprised, Jonathan. For all your reputation as a ladies' man I never thought you'd descend to physically forcing your attentions on a woman.'

'What?' More than a little discomfited, Jonathan abruptly released Maya to negotiate an unsteady step backwards. Wiping his hand across his mouth, he straightened, then looked Blaise Walker defiantly in the eye.

'Don't be daft, man! She's been making eyes at me all evening. She was practically—'

'Gagging for it?' Blaise finished smoothly.

Maya wished the ground would open up and swallow her. Humiliation made her burn with rage at the injustice of it all. Did Jonathan's famous client really believe that? She could hardly bring herself to look at Blaise Walker as she pushed back her hair, then twisted her hands anxiously together in the sensuous velvet folds of her frock.

'From where I was standing, it looked like the lady was very definitely protesting at your attentions. Why don't we just check with her to verify the matter?'

Maya found herself in the worst dilemma. If she made Jonathan look like a would-be rapist then what would that do for his client relationship with Blaise Walker? On the other hand, she had her own reputation to consider, and she was damned if she was going to trash it all in the name of public relations… She'd more or less just kissed goodbye to her job anyway.

'As I told you before, I work for Mr Faraday,' she said

evenly. 'If he mistakenly got the impression I was considering anything else by agreeing to come here this weekend then I'm sorry—but he's most definitely *wrong*.'

Colouring in spite of her determination to stay strong, Maya flicked a glance at the handsome playwright, then tore it away again before his darkly brooding stare could make her reveal even more than she'd intended. Like the fact that she'd been genuinely frightened by Jonathan's unwanted attentions. Blaise was a tall man, whose breadth of shoulder alone seemed to dominate the long, high-ceilinged corridor, and in his black tuxedo and crisp white shirt his impressive physique and confident stance instantly commanded the kind of jaw-dropping attention that was hardly commonplace in her day-to-day reality. *No wonder he'd been such a successful screen actor.* It wasn't just his looks that would hook the audience in either. The man had genuine presence.

'Well. You have your answer, my friend.'

At Blaise's mocking stare, Jonathan had the grace to look momentarily repentant. Maya saw the sudden flush of colour beneath his artificial tan.

'Too much to drink, I expect,' he mumbled, shrugging his shoulders. Then, recovering quickly, he issued Maya with a belligerent glance that spoke volumes. 'You know what it's like—women are notorious for saying one thing when they mean another. I'm sorry you didn't feel you could join us at dinner, Blaise, but perhaps we can talk about the campaign in the morning?'

'I'm an early riser,' the other man responded coolly, 'and I like to go for a run before breakfast. Seven-thirty okay with you?'

Jonathan swayed a little, as if the mere thought of getting up so early on a Sunday morning after wining and dining the night away was like asking him to swim the English Channel when he could barely swim a stroke. He touched a slightly unsteady hand to his immaculate silver hair.

'Seven-thirty's fine. I'll see you then.' Without so much as a backward glance at Maya, he made his way carefully along to the opposite end of the corridor, pushed open a door right at the end and slammed it shut behind him, the sound resonating off the walls with the same jolting impact as cannon-fire…

Allowing herself the momentary luxury of leaning against the wall in support of her quaking limbs, Maya knew her sigh was hugely relieved. She'd had a lucky escape for sure. There was only one flaw. She was dependent on Jonathan for giving her a lift home tomorrow, because he'd insisted she travel with him. She couldn't leave now even if she wanted to. Unless, of course, she was willing to blow the last of her precious month's salary on an expensive cab ride to the nearest train station—and it was so late that she doubted any trains would still be running.

'Are you all right?'

Her eyes widened a little at the unexpected concern in Blaise Walker's voice, and the warm, gravelly resonance caused an involuntarily tingle in her body that reached all the way down to her toes.

'I'm fine…thanks.'

'Tell me straight—did he completely misread the situation?'

'There wasn't a situation to begin with! Except in his own twisted little mind, that is… It certainly wasn't in mine'

Maya could have died, knowing Blaise Walker's disturbing concentrated gaze was noting everything from the plunging cleavage of her tight-fitting velvet dress to the giveaway quiver of her fulsome lower lip. Flushing angrily, she tucked a glossy strand of black hair behind her ear and jutted her chin, green eyes flashing indignant emerald fire.

'He admitted to me that he got me here under false pretences. Is it likely, under the circumstances, that I would encourage him? Look, Mr Walker…I'm just a temp who was hired to work for his PR company. I work hard to earn my pay, and at the end of the day I go home. I shouldn't have to submit to the unwanted attentions of my boss for the privilege, should I?'

Considering the question, Blaise let his avid gaze fall on the agitated rise and fall of her chest. Her lush creamy breasts looked fit to burst from her gown at any moment, and God help him but all the blood in his body marched unerringly south.

'Clearly you shouldn't have to submit to anything of the kind, Miss Hayward. By the way—you do have a first name, I presume?'

'Maya.'

She hesitated at the door of her bedroom, exhaling a long, resigned breath as she twisted the brass doorknob and pushed it open.

'I'm sorry you had to witness that distasteful little scene. I really hope you won't let it prejudice you against using Mr Faraday's company to promote you. He has some good people working for him—I shouldn't like what happened to backfire negatively on them.'

'Your concern is admirable in the light of his quite appalling behaviour. But I guess we'll just have to wait and see what the outcome will be, won't we?'

After assessing her with a maddeningly enigmatic glance, Blaise turned and started to walk back down the corridor. When he'd travelled just a couple of feet away he looked back, and with a confident little smile said, 'I don't think you'll have anything more to fear from your troublesome boss tonight. With the amount of alcohol he's consumed no doubt he'll enjoy the sleep of the dead. One word of caution, though—I'd really advise against wearing that dress at any future function, unless you're prepared to handle the very *particular* kind of attention it generates…'

Lacking the courage just then to even meet his eyes, Maya mumbled a barely audible goodnight, hurried inside her room and bolted the door firmly behind her— as hurriedly as if she'd just been chased up the corridor by a herd of wild buffalo...

CHAPTER TWO

AWAKE since dawn, Maya chose not to linger in bed. Instead she got up, took a brief hot shower, then quickly dressed. Leaving her bags momentarily in the silent corridor, where behind closed doors Jonathan and his guests were still sleeping off the excesses of the night before, she took the risk of slipping a note under her boss's door. A note that clearly outlined the reasons why she couldn't stay and act as his assistant for the rest of the weekend and concluded with telling him that as soon as they returned to the office he could expect her resignation. Then, with her heart nervously tripping, Maya carried her bags downstairs.

If truth be known she couldn't wait to get away from this house—away from her licentious boss and the cloud of deceit that had brought her there—away from his shallow moneyed friends who, when she'd been trying to make conversation, had looked right through her but had not really 'seen' her at all. It gave her an un-

comfortable sense of *déjà vu*, being around people like
that. It was too reminiscent of her childhood and those
interminable painful gatherings of her father's, with his
so-called 'friends'—acquaintances who had petted
Maya like a puppy when it suited them and told her to
get lost when it hadn't, because she was cramping their
style when they were drinking, drug-taking or trying to
seduce someone.

Right now all she wanted was to return to her own
little place, to what was comforting and familiar. She
would have said to what was safe too, but since Maya
had almost never experienced such a condition she bit
her lip on the thought and shelved it away in some clan-
destine corner of her mind, where she would endeavour
to forget about it for a while.

'So…I'm not the only early riser around here, I see.'

Intent on leafing through the Yellow Pages she'd
found in the hallway for a cab number, Maya glanced
round, startled at the appearance of the owner of that
low, provocative male voice. *Lord, have mercy!*

Dressed from head to toe in enigmatic black, Blaise
Walker resembled a dangerous secret fantasy come to
blood-pounding, heart-racing life, with his dark gold
hair swept sleekly back from his strong sculpted face
and his sizzling bold glance that now, in the light of day,
she saw was a magnetic Mediterranean blue. She
couldn't attest to breathing at all as she stared back at
him, but for several dizzying seconds the same roaring

exhilaration pounded through her bloodstream that she imagined a Formula One driver must experience when he'd successfully negotiated a treacherous bend at devastating speed...

'Good morning. I'm always up early, I'm afraid... I'm not one of those people who can lie in bed 'til late. Besides...' sensing heat suffuse her, Maya defied any woman with a libido to say the word 'bed' in front of a gorgeous male specimen like Blaise Walker and *not* be consumed with heat '...just as soon as I can get a cab I'm making my way home.'

'So you've decided not to stay?'

'To be honest, I don't think that would be a very good idea—and I think my boss would probably agree. I don't doubt he can't wait to be rid of me after last night.'

'You mean because you didn't play along with his drunken and rather crass attempt at seduction?'

Casually sliding a hand into one of his trouser pockets, Blaise moved with compelling masculine grace towards Maya. A tantalising smile played round his well-cut lips that might have been mockery, curiosity, or perhaps even sympathy—who knew? That aside, his blunt description brought back afresh the sickening fear that had shuddered through her when Jonathan had been leering down into her cleavage and pinning her up against the wall.

'You call that seduction? It was horrible! Just horrible! He had no right to—' Her face flaming with embarrassment and a silent deepening fury at her boss's totally reprehensible and rough treatment of her, Maya raked a shaky hand through her newly washed hair. 'He'll be doubly embarrassed that you saw it happen. I expect he'll also be furious that I rejected him. I'd rather not stay here and find out his reaction, to tell you the truth.'

Moving her still trembling fingers down the appropriate thin page of the phone book, she located a number, then glanced back at the six-feet-something of powerfully arresting, hard-muscled male standing less than a foot away from her. Every cell in her body seemed to be drowning in the most compelling, exquisitely *painful* awareness of him, and she didn't feel a bit prepared to deal with the fact.

Feeling as if his sharp gaze saw every self-conscious move she made, she turned to lay the book back down on the polished chiffonier.

'I'd better phone for a cab. Excuse me…'

'Where do you need a lift to?'

'The nearest station.'

'To catch a train to where? London?'

'Yes…Camden.'

'Don't bother phoning a cab. I'll take you.'

'But the nearest station is fifteen miles away! What about Jonathan?'

'What about him?'

'Don't you and he have a meeting this morning?'

The blue eyes that reminded Maya of perfectly still

twin oceans that could no doubt seethe and turn stormy along with the best of deceptively calm seas stared back at her, as if the agreed meeting was of very little account indeed. Knowing from Jonathan's assistant Caroline what mercenary methods her boss regularly employed in order for his agency to represent the 'hot' names of the moment when up against the competition, Maya couldn't help but wonder what her boss had done to pull off this particular coup. In the world of theatre Blaise Walker's name was definitely hotter than hot. She knew that was true because she regularly scanned the Entertainment and Arts pages of the papers, to see what was on in the West End, and she had read the fulsome and glowing accolades his work commanded as well as seeing the 'Sold Out' notices on the billboards.

But now she worried that if Blaise Walker didn't make his meeting with Jonathan because he had given her a lift to the station then Jonathan would no doubt hold her completely responsible. Retribution in some form or other would quickly follow...maybe even manifesting itself in his refusal to give her a reference for her next job with her employment agency. It would be highly unfair and irregular, in light of Maya's unblemished employment record, but Jonathan was more than capable of it—and *worse*.

'I'll ring him later. I'm pretty sure our Mr Faraday won't lift his head off the pillow until lunchtime at least...*if* even then,' Blaise remarked nonchalantly, dropping his hands to his hips. 'In any case, after what I witnessed last night, any inclination I may have had to let your boss do my PR has definitely disappeared. One hears things about people. As a rule I don't believe in listening to gossip, but having seen for myself the way the man conducts himself I've come to realise that much of the talk about him is probably quite close to the truth. The meeting I do eventually have with him won't be the one he was hoping for, I'm afraid. Now… are these all your bags?'

Staring uncomfortably down at her soft canvas hold-all, and the small leather tote bag that housed amongst other things her make-up, book and reading glasses, Maya was genuinely taken aback at the idea that Blaise had deplored Jonathan's treatment of her and was showing his displeasure by withdrawing his agreement to let his agency do his publicity. She realised she'd been nursing a real fear that he would side with her boss when it came to believing any attractive woman that worked for him was fair game. But now she also wrestled with the idea of allowing a man she barely knew, and who could potentially turn out to be just like some of those mercenary acquaintances of her father's—self-obsessed and making no bones about going after what they wanted no matter *who* they might hurt in the process—to drive her home.

Lifting her concerned emerald gaze to his, she frowned.

'You really don't have to bother, Mr Walker—'

'Blaise,' he insisted.

'It's easy enough for me to get a cab. At least then I won't disturb the rest of your weekend.'

'Oh, but you *have* disturbed me, Maya,' he answered enigmatically, a glint in his eyes that made her insides clench, 'but that's hardly your fault. Come on—let's get you to the station. I'll carry your bags.'

'Really…' Still unsure, she grimaced. 'It might be better in the long run if I just phoned for a cab.'

'If you're worried that I might have a tendency to behave in any way, shape or form like your disreputable boss then please let me assure you right now your concerns are groundless. I personally like my women willing, and I've never had to force one into my bed yet!'

Reddening at his frank confession, Maya shrugged and attempted a smile. 'Okay…'

Outside, a watery sun had broken through the early-morning clouds, and on the gravel drive where Jonathan's esteemed guests had parked a selection of gleaming and expensive vehicles Blaise Walker headed for a dazzling fire-engine-red classic open-topped MG sports car. Go-to-hell red, as her father had used to call that particular shade. Maya fielded the unexpected memory, but wasn't quick enough to suppress the little knot of tension that squeezed inside her.

Instantly Blaise picked up on her disquiet. 'Is anything the matter? Perhaps you were expecting something a little more sedate for your ride to the station?'

'I had no expectations at all,' Maya replied evenly. 'I'm just grateful for the lift.'

He replaced his concern with a captivating grin, and the sight brought the same sense of wonder with it to Maya as reaching the end of a frightening rollercoaster ride and realising that you'd survived. A feeling of totally giddy exhilaration flooded her body. In all her twenty-five years on the planet she'd *never* witnessed a smile as dazzling or as wildly, extraordinarily beautiful as that.

'You might want to find something to tie your hair back with,' Blaise suggested now. 'Could get a little windswept otherwise.'

Checking through her tote as he opened the rather compact boot in order to deposit her luggage, and seeing his own expensive bag ensconced there—*was he leaving this morning too?*—Maya produced a slender multi-coloured chiffon scarf and proceeded to tie her flowing dark hair up into a loosely fashioned ponytail.

'That okay?'

'You look adorable.' Her companion grinned. 'Get in and make yourself comfortable. The door's unlocked.'

Folding her long-legged, slender, jean-clad frame into the passenger seat, Maya relaxed as far as she was able in the small space provided. Easing back into the softly luxurious leather seat, she silently admired the immaculate burr walnut veneer that covered the dash and centre console, and the amazing craftsmanship that had produced what her father had once informed her was one of the country's bestselling sports cars *ever*.

He should have known, because when she was little he had owned two of them—one in red, like this, and another in black. *Of course they were long gone now.* Sold to help pay off some of the horrendous debts his wildly reckless lifestyle had accrued...

Hearing the lid of the boot slam, she turned to see Blaise lower his own tall, athletic, black-clad frame into the driver's seat. Even though his legs were long, like hers, Maya was quietly amazed at how effortless he made every movement look...like a sublime symphony...every note in perfect accord and nothing remotely out of sync. A waft of quietly stirring aftershave imbued with sultry notes of sandalwood and musk assailed senses already tested to their limit by his charismatic presence. She tried to steel herself against it.

'This is a concourse model, isn't it?' she commented, her fingertips lightly touching the walnut veneer on the dash.

'Yes, it is. It's an original model, but I paid a small fortune to get everything restored down to the last nut and bolt back to the way it was. You know about classic cars?' her companion asked in surprise.

'Not really. I just knew someone once who had a model like this.' Maya stared out through the windscreen instead of into the disturbing blue eyes that seemed to be playing such havoc with her insides. The huskily soft chuckle beside her was equally disconcerting.

'You probably know a lot more than you're admitting, right? That's okay... I don't mind you being a woman of mystery. It simply makes me want to get to know you even more.'

He shouldn't have been surprised, but she was even more alluring and beautiful dressed in jeans and a simple white cotton shirt than she'd been in that eye-popping black dress that had paid such mouthwatering homage to her curves last night. And that dress had caused him one *hell* of a sleepless night, he recalled now, his hands tightening on the MG's steering wheel. Seeing Jonathan Faraday's drunken paws all over her had also been a factor in ensuring Blaise's sleep was fitful. *He had been a breath away from laying the man out flat.* Maya had clearly been frightened by Faraday's clumsy inebriated attentions, and all his latent protective instincts towards women had rushed to the fore. She would have had only to indicate to him by a mere glance that she wanted him to step in and her licentious boss would have been nursing much more than a hangover this morning.

When he was about ten years old, Blaise's actor father had struck his mother savagely across the face during one of their many bitter rows—an event that, after that shocking first time, had become a more or less regular feature of his childhood, he was sorry to say. *Blaise had leapt on him, kicking and screaming.* He had truly wanted to kill him at that moment. The same strong feelings of fury and resentment had roared through his bloodstream last night in the corridor, when he'd seen Jonathan behave like some despicable Neanderthal.

Now Blaise realised just how much the bewitching Maya Hayward had been on his mind since she'd inadvertently burst in on him in the drawing room last evening, leaving a trail of sexy perfume in her wake and stirring the kind of fantasies that would be strictly rated 'adults only'. He definitely wanted to get to know her better. It had been quite some time since he'd enjoyed an exciting affair, and this could potentially be his most exciting liaison yet.

When he'd found her in the hall searching through the phonebook the pure raw desire that had coursed through him had been fierce enough to almost make him stumble. Now he realised Jonathan Faraday's loss was definitely his *gain*, and he made no apology for the mercenary-sounding realisation whatsoever...

At some point during the journey it started to rain, and Blaise had no choice but to put the MG's top up. His bewitching passenger didn't even notice, however. To his surprise and amusement she'd fallen asleep—head on one side and her soft breathing making him feel strangely calm and peaceful—as he smoothly steered the vehicle onto the motorway heading towards London. *Almost straight away he had decided he would forgo the ride to the station and take her all the way home instead.* The faintest suggestion of a smile touched his lips. It had been worth staying at Faraday's house last night to now have the opportunity that had opened up to him. The only possible impediment to him getting to know Maya more intimately, he mused, was if there was a man in her life already. The idea caused a totally disproportionate stab of jealousy to slice through his middle.

Glancing sidelong at her now, he let his gaze skim the arresting, fulsome curve of her breast nestling beneath crisp white cotton, and the long, slender length of her denim-clad thigh. The hot, sweet need that immediately surged through Blaise's bloodstream made him clench his jaw to contain it, and it was only out of pure necessity and commonsense that he returned his full attention back to the road…

She felt warm and safe, and the sound of the rain pattering on the roof somehow gave her a wonderful sense of inviolability and protection. The experience was so delicious that Maya just wanted to stay there, eyes shut tight against the world, for a little while longer, reluctant to surface from sleep and even face the day at all…

But suddenly a strongly disturbing instinct made her peer out from beneath her drowsy lids—only to find that she wasn't in her bed at home, but in a car, being driven on the motorway at quite a lick in the outside lane. Beside her was a man with the chiselled profile of a model. Her heart pounded in shock.

'How long have I been asleep?' Her voice was husky and she sounded like someone else. Sitting up straight, she adjusted her previously cramped position with a relieved groan.

'Practically since we started out.' A fleeting grin appeared on her companion's carved, compelling features.

Maya stared. 'Was the station closed or something?'

'No. It wasn't closed. I just decided to take you to London myself. It's no big deal. I came to the conclusion that I should head home to Primrose Hill anyway, so it's not too far out of my way.'

'You have a place in London too? I thought Jonathan told me you lived in Northumberland?'

'I do. But when I'm working at the theatre it makes sense to stay in town. A play of mine has just completed a six-month run and will soon be on its way to Broadway, so I'll be going back to Northumberland in the meantime to rest and continue working on my latest project. Whereabouts in Camden are you situated?'

Maya told him, with not a little sense of unreality in her voice. Her softly shaped dark brows drew together in genuine puzzlement.

'I can't believe I fell asleep like that. It must have been all that upset last night. I don't think I slept a wink afterwards, to tell you the truth. But to fall asleep with someone I hardly even know driving me…that's a first!'

Briefly Blaise turned his head to survey her. 'I hope we can very soon rectify the fact that you hardly know me, Maya. It should be fairly obvious to you by now that I'd very much like to see you again?'

She fell silent for a moment. 'You mean like on a date?'

Digesting this bombshell, twin feelings of surprise and apprehension flooded her.

'Is that so shocking?' Directing the MG into a long line of traffic heading towards Greenwich, Blaise smiled.

'Not shocking, exactly…but I am surprised, yes.'

'And are you pleased or *not* pleased about it? Maybe you're seeing someone already?' he fished.

It had been two years since Maya had been in a relationship. A relationship in which her trust in someone had been utterly violated. The memory was still liable to churn her guts from time to time whenever she thought about it.

'I'm not seeing anyone else. But then I'm not really interested in dating at the moment. Particularly as I've probably just talked myself out of a job! There's no guarantee that my agency will have another position for me straight away, and I might have to look round other places as well.'

'Do you enjoy working for Faraday?' Blaise's voice was definitely disgruntled.

'Not for him personally…but I have enjoyed working with my fellow colleagues and the job itself.'

'Well, then, let's not jump the gun here, shall we?'

'What do you mean?'

'There hasn't been any mention of you being let go yet, has there?'

'No, but—'

'Then why don't you cross that bridge when you come to it? Right now it's all hypothetical. If you really want to keep your job then I'll have a word with Faraday myself and tell him it was *me* that made you leave early. There shouldn't be a problem. Although why you would want to work anywhere *near* the man is beyond me!'

'It's kind of you, but you don't need to talk to him on my behalf. Besides…' Maya shrugged awkwardly. 'I left him a note telling him that I couldn't work for him any longer after what happened, and if I take back what I said to try and ameliorate the situation then no doubt he'll endeavour to make my life as miserable as possible as a punishment. No…it's probably for the best that I leave. I wasn't exactly ecstatic at being asked to work for a PR agency anyway.'

'Why was that?'

'I'm just not mad about celebrity culture, I suppose.'

'Can't say I blame you.' Blaise grimaced a little. 'But if you're going to be free for a while then you'll have time to make a date with me to go out to dinner…right?'

CHAPTER THREE

MAYA had directed Blaise to pull up in front of a slim four-storeyed house in a narrow side-street not far from Camden Lock. The area was a Mecca for locals and tourists, flocking to the outdoor and indoor markets selling an eclectic mix of crafts, jewellery, music, clothing and artefacts from all round the world. The soft late summer rain had long since ceased, and the sun had made a welcome reappearance. With the sports car's top rolled down again it was easy to detect the exotic aromas of food, incense and the other myriad scents that permeated the air.

The surrounding pavements and roads were heaving with cars and people, and it had taken quite some time to negotiate the busy, packed streets to reach Maya's address. But now they were there, and Blaise realised his stomach was clenched tight as a drum as he lifted her bags from the boot of the car, waiting expectantly— not to mention a little *impatiently*—for her to finally address the question of a dinner date. He could already tell by the vibes he was getting that she had no intention of inviting him in for a coffee or anything like that and, resigning himself to the fact, he had to irritably bite back his frustration.

'Well…thanks so much for driving me all the way home. It was above and beyond the call of duty and very sweet of you.'

Sweet? Blaise almost choked on the ironic laughter that bubbled up inside him. *Should he regard such a comment as a compliment, or as a sign that he'd definitely lost his touch?* Smiling ruefully at the lovely brunette in front of him, he couldn't help noticing the anxiety reflected in her mesmerising green gaze, and he was intensely curious as to the cause of it. *Had some other jerk like Faraday messed around with her? Hurt her, perhaps?* The knot in his stomach gripped even tighter.

'It was my pleasure. Perhaps you'll think about meeting up again some time soon?' He was fishing in his wallet for a business card. 'I'll be in London at least until the end of next week. After that I'm returning to Hexham.'

'Hexham?'

'It's a market town near where I live in Northumberland.'

She took the card he proffered and folded it in her hand without so much as a glance. 'I will. I'll definitely think about it.'

Would she? Contemplating that she might *not* was

definitely a massive blow to Blaise's pride. To practically be given the brush-off by a woman he'd made it more than clear that he liked was something that had never happened before, and was *not* an experience he was in a hurry to replicate.

'Well…' he shrugged his powerful shoulders with pretended good humour '…that's all I can ask. Take care of yourself, and don't worry about Faraday. You'll have no problem finding another position—I'm sure of it. And if you do—give me a call and I'll see what I can do.' Lightly he clasped her arms, sensing her bewitching perfume sensually invading him. Then he kissed her continental style, on both cheeks, and moved away. 'Goodbye, Maya.'

'Goodbye. Drive safely.'

As he gunned the engine and roared away from the kerb, Blaise saw in his rearview mirror that she stood on the pavement, watching him. Grimly he clenched his jaw, ruthlessly brushing aside any doubt or imagined obstacles that might arise to prevent him seeing her. Of *course* he would see her again! Now that he knew where she lived, why the hell should he *not*?

For the first time since setting eyes on Blaise Walker that morning Maya finally felt as if she could breathe freely again. Never before had a man unsettled her and yet perversely commanded her attention quite as much. It seriously troubled her. No doubt if her friends found out he'd given her a lift home they'd think she was *mad* for not agreeing to a date! But then none of them had experienced what Maya had experienced in associating with people from similar privileged circumstances. People who were part of an elite, almost *oppressive* circle of wealth, fame and privilege that was a million light years from the kind of ordinary lives Maya and her friends lived... *Wolves in sheep's clothing*, as her young teenage self had thought of them. All glitz on the outside but frighteningly shallow and cruel within.

She realised she was definitely apprehensive that Blaise could potentially turn out to be like that. No doubt her friends would be *more* than impressed with his dazzling good-looks, achievements and wealth if they were in her shoes—but then they still thought that money and fame were some kind of Holy Grail to instant happiness while Maya sadly knew different.

With a sigh that was part relief at getting away from that horrible weekend party and—*shockingly* disturbingly—part lingering regret that she'd more or less indicated to Blaise that she wasn't at all interested in going out on a date with him, she let herself into the tiny studio flat, dropped her bags onto the rush-matted floor and moved across the room to open the window and let in some fresh air.

As she turned back to survey the small domain that was both her living room and her sleeping quarters, when she turned down the functional bed-settee each night, Maya's gaze alighted on the medium-sized portrait hanging on the opposite wall. *It was a painting of herself at fourteen...* Her dark hair was in thick plaited ropes, and there was an expression in her eyes that easily reflected the painful shadows in her teenage heart. It had been painted at her father's insistence, during one of his more mellow periods. A rare time when he hadn't been drinking and partying into the early hours and had perhaps had an inkling of his daughter's deep unhappiness at his neglect of her.

'Smile, darling!' he had coaxed from behind the easel that had been permanently set up in what had once been the dining room of the grand Georgian residence they'd lived in. The space had been commandeered as her father's studio due to the exceptional quality of the light that had flooded in through the huge windows.

'I don't feel like smiling,' Maya had answered, in typical sulky teenage fashion but with an ache in her heart big enough to fill an ocean.

The portrait had turned out to be the last picture her father had ever painted.

After that, more late-night drug- and drink-fuelled parties had beckoned, with his so-called 'friends', and there had been no more mellow periods ever again. Three years after that he'd taken his own life, and at seventeen Maya had lost her home as well as her father.

Impatient at the deeply disturbing memories that made her feel heavy as lead, she glanced at the time on her watch, making a decision. She would forgo unpacking her stuff and instead go into Camden Market and have a coffee at her friend Diego's coffee bar. She'd sit and scan the Sunday newspapers, deliberately bypassing the doom-laden stories for the lighter ones, and instead of letting her mind be racked with regret and pain she'd watch the endlessly interesting characters that came and went in the market, imagining what *their* lives were like instead of dwelling on her own, and the day could just unfold however it willed…

'What do you mean, give her a job?'

Jane Eddington—Blaise's quick-minded, sharp-suited American agent—threw Blaise one of her most piercing and suspicious glances over the top of her high-fashion reading glasses.

'Someone really *has* stirred your sugar, honey, haven't they? You've never gone this far before in order to get a woman into bed! Don't tell me there exists in the world a female who *can* actually resist your charms, Blaise—myriad and devastating though they are?'

'Your encroaching years are making you cynical, Jane…and it doesn't suit you,' Blaise countered with a scowl.

'I'll ignore that distinctly ungentlemanly remark and simply say this: you've just spent the past twenty minutes verbally blasting Jonathan Faraday *again* for being an out-and-out sleaze and a snake for trying to coerce this girl into bed against her will, and now you're doing the same…albeit more covertly…by asking me to give her a job just so you can conveniently call on her whenever the mood takes you!'

'Please don't insult me by suggesting I'm remotely like that poor excuse for a human being! He's put Maya in an untenable position and practically forced her to resign. She really does need a job and I want you to hire her. You're always saying you need extra help around here.'

'Maya? Is that her name?'

With a mocking little smile, Jane adjusted her glasses and met the piercing azure glance of the answer to every woman's prayer currently perching his Savile Row-suited, perfectly taut male bottom on the edge of her desk.

'You know that name means illusion, don't you? Perhaps you've dreamt the lady up out of pure sexual frustration and the fact that it's been…what? At least six months since your last affair?'

With an impatient sigh Blaise shook his head and pushed to his feet. 'You know far too much about me, and it's not healthy.'

'Look, darling… I really would like to help you out, but I hired a girl only just last week. She starts on Monday.' With a glance that was perfectly guileless, Jane removed her glasses, laid them down amongst the detritus of paperwork on her desk and with the air of an old-fashioned headmistress folded her arms.

'What's her name?' asked Blaise.

'I forget. I know I've written it down somewhere...'
She waved her hand vaguely towards the pile of paperwork in front of her.

'Hmm... Well, if you won't do me this one small
favour and employ Maya at the agency then I'll simply
have to suggest that she comes and works for me personally. No doubt there are at least a dozen jobs she can
do to help me out. As you know, I've started the new
play, and so as long as she has an inkling of how to do
research, type and make the odd cup of coffee she'll
probably work out just fine.'

'And that's *really* all that you want her to do for you,
is it, Blaise?'

Despite the impatience that had been building inside
him like a pressure-cooker for the last few days—
because it had been *that* long since he'd last set eyes on
Maya and no phone call from her had been forthcoming—he sensed a devilish smile hitch the corners of his
lips upwards. '*Darling,*' he drawled sarcastically, 'I
really don't think it's any of your damn business!'

Glasses perched firmly back on her nose again, Jane
shot to her feet with a deep frown between her perfectly
arched slim brows.

'You mean you'd really take her to the wilds of
Northumberland with you? In the five years I've been
your agent I've never known you to take a woman up
there—especially when you're working!'

For answer, Blaise tunnelled his fingers through the

sleek strands of his dark gold hair and strode casually across to the door.

'They say there's a first time for everything. I'll be in touch. Hope your new girl works out okay. I'll look forward to meeting her when I get back to London.'

With a knowing little smile and a mocking salute, he abruptly turned and went out through the door...

'Oh...it's you!'

Staring back into the deep blue eyes of one of the country's finest playwrights as he stood casually on her doorstep, looking for all the world as if he made a habit of calling on her at odd hours of the day or night, was like being hypnotised. Maya sensed her heart clang loudly in alarm. Clutching the sides of her short towelling robe tightly together, and with her long hair still dripping from her shower, she hardly knew what to say or think. She couldn't deny that the man had been on her mind pretty much constantly since he'd given her a lift home that disastrous weekend, but quite frankly finding him on her doorstep was as startling as if Prince William or Harry had unexpectedly made her a visit!

'Yes, it's me.' He grinned, unabashed. 'How are you?'

'I'm—I'm fine...surprised to see you, that's all.'

He considered this for a long moment, before flashing Maya another disturbing smile. 'And you don't like being taken by surprise, I take it?'

'I don't know. I mean—'

'I'd like a word with you, if I may? Can I come in?'

'Well, I—'

'You're not about to leave for work, are you? I thought as it was after ten you would have left by now if you were going.'

'I wasn't planning on going anywhere today other than the supermarket, for some groceries. And as for going to work... Jonathan Faraday decided not to wait for Monday to accept my resignation, but rang me on Sunday night instead, to suggest that I didn't bother to go back at all.' Shrugging off the wave of anger that arose inside her at the crude, almost aggressive way Jonathan had spoken to her, as if this whole sorry mess was *her* fault, Maya stood up a little straighter as she sensed her shoulders start to slump.

'Anyway, I decided to give myself the week off to take stock of things. I've told the agency I'll start back at work next Monday.'

'You know you could doubtless sue him for unfair dismissal, citing sexual harassment?'

'And give myself even more grief?' Maya shook her head with a bitter little laugh. 'He's probably done me a favour. At least I won't have to put up with his sleazy behaviour any more!'

The implacable look on her visitor's mesmerising face gave her no clue as to his thoughts right then, and Maya sensed her stomach sink. *Did he think she was a fool for not putting up more of a fight for her rights than she had?* Right then she could have *wept* at the injustice of it all. No matter how hard women had fought for equality it was still a man's world when all was said and done—and didn't birds of a feather flock together?

'I'd still like to come in, if that's okay? I promise this won't take long. I can see that my timing could have been a bit better.'

'I was in the shower when you rang the bell.'

'So it appears.'

His definitely interested gaze made a casually bold appraisal of Maya's partially clothed state. *It was as though the beam of a red-hot laser touched her everywhere at once.* In contrast, an icy drip of water slid down the back of her neck from her wet hair and caused a convulsive shiver.

'You'd better come up, then. You'll have to let me finish dressing and drying my hair before we talk.'

'Don't feel you have to do that on my account.'

His huskily voiced drawl made another wave of heat submerge Maya, and she quickly turned back inside the house, before he could witness the fierce, revealing blush that scorched her cheeks, and headed up the stairs. Her teeth nibbling worriedly on her lower lip, she wished she could relax about Blaise being right behind her, but it was seriously challenging knowing his gaze was doubtless lingering on the natural sway of her shapely hips, and he would be fully aware that beneath her robe she was as bare as the day she was born...

* * *

Having reluctantly watched his very diverting hostess disappear into a bathroom on the landing, and having been directed by her to enter the room next to it, Blaise breathed out to try and ease some of the inevitable tension that had gathered inside his chest. He knew he was taking a risk, forcing the issue rather than waiting for Maya to ring him, but damn it he was going back up north the day after tomorrow, and he simply couldn't wait any longer for a phone call that—going by the deafening silence of the week—was probably not even forthcoming. It wasn't his style to chase a woman, but it was as if something stronger than his own will—*some force of nature he could not ignore*—was now in charge where this girl was concerned. It compelled him all the more to find out why.

Noticing a little pottery vase of yellow and white freesias on the mantelpiece above a small fireplace swept meticulously clean, Blaise briefly bent his head to sniff their distinctive piquant scent. Glancing round, he interestedly examined the rest of the room. *Not that there was a lot to see.* A simple light brown couch, submerged beneath a veritable bazaar of silky cushions in varying shades of purple and red, faced an armchair that looked like a refugee from a charity shop. With its frayed arms and flattened seat, it had definitely seen better days. Apart from a small pine wardrobe tucked away in a corner, and a stout oak bookcase with its shelves literally crammed with paperbacks and hard-backs, Maya's furniture was very slim pickings indeed.

He sensed a frown forming. He knew stagehands at the theatre who lived more luxuriously than this! As he released a sigh, his gaze inadvertently collided with the most stunning portrait of a young girl. Apart from a couple of film posters it was the only picture in the room. Even at a distance he could see it was a sublime work. Moving closer, Blaise realised two things that made his heart almost jump out of his chest. Firstly, the portrait was of a teenaged Maya—a very vulnerable-looking and beautiful Maya, on the cusp of young wom-anhood—and secondly, the artist who had painted it, confirmed by the scrawled name at the very bottom right-hand corner, was only one of a handful of British artists whose work could literally command *millions*.

Blaise should know, because he was the envied owner of one of his paintings himself. A searing, frank depiction of a well-known actor his father had mentored, it had captured him on stage during dress re-hearsals for the play that had made his name. It had been left to Blaise by his parents after they'd passed away, and it hung in pride of place at his house in the North. He could have sold it a thousand times over, such was the worldwide demand for this particular artist's work. and he'd long craved to own another one.

Rubbing a troubled and curious hand round the back of his shirt-collar, he felt the skin between his brows pucker again. *How had Maya come to know such an acclaimed artist and sit for him?* More than that, why was she living in a one-roomed studio flat in a hardly prosperous area of Camden when she had in her possession a portrait that was without a doubt…*priceless*?

The noisy whirr of a hairdryer briefly distracted him. Casting a quick glance over his shoulder, Blaise returned his stunned attention back to the portrait. Captivating didn't come close to describing it. Even if you didn't know the girl whose cat-like almond-shaped green eyes gazed back at you with the kind of wounded glance that made a man feel personally responsible for whatever had hurt her, and broke something open inside him that he'd probably prefer *not* to have disturbed, you'd know you were witnessing something quite *extraordinary*.

The door opened and the sitter for the portrait—now clothed in light blue denims and an ethnic patterned silk top, with her pretty feet disturbingly bare—ventured an uncertain smile in his direction. The second her shy glance met his, a deep, magnetic tug of pure, undiluted sexual awareness made everything inside Blaise clench hard.

'This is you…right?' Fielding the sensual heat that now gripped him with a vengeance, he indicated the painting he'd been studying. Her tentative smile vanished.

'Yes.'

'The artist is world renowned…how did you come to sit for him? Was he a friend of your family's, perhaps?'

Maya's ensuing heavy sigh was laced with irritation.

'People are always so impressed by fame and celebrity, aren't they? It doesn't always follow that the person concerned is the best example of a decent person you could know or even *like*. Why don't people ever think about that? Because in my book that's the thing that really counts.'

CHAPTER FOUR

'I HEARD that Alistair Devereaux had his challenges. He must have had to take his own life.'

Maya winced. 'So you know about that?'

'He was probably one of the most inspirational and influential artists of his generation. How could I *not* have known that he'd killed himself?' Blaise's brow creased. 'But you still haven't told me how you came to sit for him.'

Eight years he had been gone, but the pain never seemed to lessen... Maya experienced the familiar tumult of despair and shuddering shock that she always felt when the subject of her father's death came up, and she restlessly linked and unlinked her hands as she mentally stumbled to stay upright against the great swell of hurt that surfaced in her heart. She could see that Blaise was clearly puzzling over how on earth someone like her could have sat for one of the country's most illustrious artists, and she couldn't help resenting the unspoken judgement that out of habit she naturally assumed.

'He was my father.' An edge of defiance under-
lined her tone.

'Your *father*?' Genuinely taken aback, Blaise stared.

'That's right.'

'I wasn't aware that he'd left children behind.'

'Well, he did…*me*.'

'But your name's Hayward, isn't it?'

'After he died I started using my mother's maiden
name.' Maya lowered herself into the armchair because
her legs suddenly felt disconcertingly wobbly. Visitors to
her humble little home inevitably remarked on the
portrait—why should Blaise Walker be any different? *The
picture was the only beautifully crafted thing in the room,
and therefore it was bound to draw attention.* But most of
her friends didn't even know who the artist was, and Maya
had not been in a particular hurry to enlighten them.

Now, linking hands that were suddenly icy, she
watched silently as her enigmatic visitor lowered his
tall, fit frame onto the couch, moved cushions out of the
way to get comfortable, then briefly speared his fingers
through his hair.

'Why? Because it was difficult to live with the attention from the press and the public?' Blaise speculated.

'Something like that.'

'What about your mother? Presumably she must
have outlived him?'

'No. She died when I was four. I hardly remember her.'

'That's tough.'

Silence, then… 'So you were left on your own?'

'I managed.' Embarrassment was crawling over her skin with debilitating heat, and Maya shrugged. Then, riding the crest of her unease, she observed her handsome visitor with a steely look. She'd had enough of this awkward exchange, and the truth was after the week she'd just had she was in no mood for playing games with anyone—*least* of all with another man who was possibly only after one thing.

'I don't mean to be rude, but what do you want with me, Mr Walker? You must be a very busy man, and it's really not clear to me why you're here.'

Meeting her gaze equally frankly, Blaise leant forward to rest his elbows on his knees. 'I was hoping you'd call,' he said.

A flame of hope flickered and blazed with the strongest compulsion in Maya's heart. *Then cynicism and hurt moved swiftly in to douse it.*

'I didn't call because I'm not interested in seeing anyone at the moment… To be absolutely blunt with you it's the very last thing I need! The only thing I really need right now is—'

Her guest cut across what she'd been going to say with that devastating smile of his—the one that seemed to have the disturbing ability to suspend her thoughts and dive deep down into her most secret core, awakening every fragile dream and hope that slumbered there, making them flare into vibrant and dangerous life again.

'How do you know that I'm not the perfect answer to what you need if you don't even give me a chance?'

Oh, he was good. For a fleeting, vulnerable moment Maya almost wanted to give him that chance—but then she quickly remembered who he was. *Hadn't she had enough examples of men in the arts like him, who completely disregarded women's feelings and lied to them as easily as breathing?* Artists were a selfish, self-obsessed breed. She'd learned that to her cost…her father being a case in point. His constant lies and unfulfilled promises about taking care of her had demolished every bit of trust she'd had, and it had been obvious that he preferred to put his work and so-called friends first. She was under no illusions about what men like him could or couldn't deliver when it came to close personal relationships.

Now, as she levelled her glance at Blaise, every single one of her defences slammed and then double-locked into place.

'You have no idea what I need…none! But I'll tell you this much—it isn't another man who'll lie to me and make promises he has no intention of keeping! And it isn't a man who hasn't the slightest inkling of who I really am and…worse than that…can't see past what I look like to even trouble to find out!'

'Maybe you've just been seeing the wrong kind of men, Maya.'

'And maybe we should just change the subject.'

Pushing to her feet, she crossed the room to a curtained-off area that secluded the small confined space that was the kitchen.

'Do you want some tea or coffee? I have fruit tea if you don't want caffeine.'

Her heart still thudding with emotion, she splashed water into the kettle and then inserted the plug into the wall socket. She sensed a tangible, perturbing shift in the air with the realisation that Blaise had stepped up behind her.

'I didn't come here to distress you,' he said, quiet-voiced, and it was as though sensuous strokes from the softest sable brush had skimmed across Maya's skin. A deeply sensual pull in the pit of her stomach made her long to close her eyes, so that she could revel in the pleasure of it for a little while longer.

'You told me you were intending to quit Faraday's agency and, apart from wanting to see you again, I came here to offer you a job.'

She turned at that and blinked at him, disconcerted to find him suddenly so close. In those electrifying few moments as she gazed at him every thought in her head was emphatically silenced—even the one that insisted she wasn't interested in dating anyone...*especially* someone like Blaise Walker, whose looks and credentials were too reminiscent of her father's phoney celebrity friends all those years ago and threatened to awaken ghosts she'd prefer to let lie dormant.

'A…a job?' she echoed, unable to stem the sudden quaver in her voice.

'I need a personal assistant for a few weeks to help me gather information for my new play. I'll be working from my house in Northumberland, so if you don't mind being away from London for a while, the job's yours.'

'And why would you offer *me* such a job? You must know people who are far more qualified and capable, I'm sure.'

'If you must know, I spoke to someone at the temp agency you work for and they told me you're hard-working, quick to learn and extremely reliable.'

Maya knew she was well liked at the agency, and that she did indeed do her job well, but it was still a bit of a shock to learn that Blaise had personally spoken to someone to discover that for himself.

'And this job you're offering…it's on the level, as they say? I mean…' she flinched a little '…you're not just stringing me along?'

'It's a real bona fide job, Maya.' He dropped his hands to his hips and one corner of his mouth nudged fleetingly towards a smile. 'And I swear I'm not stringing you along. In fact, if you want, I'll give you my agent's number and you can verify it with her. Her name's Jane Eddington and her office is in Shaftesbury Avenue. She's been a theatrical agent for years and is well known in the business.'

'I believe you… If you went to so much trouble to find out if I could do the job then I don't think I need to check.'

There was a brief look of surprise on his face, then his features seemed to relax.

'To put you in the picture, the play I'm writing has a strong historical context and needs quite a bit of research. I normally get secretarial help via Jane, but I've decided to try a different approach this time. To have someone I can directly call upon for help who's staying in the house with me while I'm writing makes much more sense.'

'I see.' Maya swept some long strands of silky, still slightly damp hair behind her ear. *To get away from London for a while, away from the noise and constant restless movement of people and traffic, definitely had its allure.* But she didn't doubt it wouldn't be easy taking on this particular assignment. She already sensed a powerful magnetic pull between herself and Blaise, and that revelation alone potentially signalled the sort of emotional turmoil she should definitely be running a mile from, given her history.

But on the other hand she really *did* need a job, and it had been a long time since any kind of lucky break at all had knocked on her door.

'It sounds like the work might be very interesting,' she admitted cautiously, 'and frankly it's a much more appealing prospect than sitting by the phone waiting for the agency to ring.' She forced herself to gaze steadily back into the long-lashed blue eyes that confronted her...at all that sculpted, breathless masculine beauty and burning intelligence…and knew with sudden stunning clarity that she would have to doubly strengthen her emotional armour against falling for such an incredible man. Even now Maya's heart throbbed with anxiety.

'Does that signify a yes or a no?' Blaise enquired, a definite hint of impatience in his tone. 'I have to have your answer today, I'm afraid. I'm going back the day after tomorrow.'

'What kind of remuneration are you offering?' she asked, dry-mouthed, uneasy at discussing money—but she had living costs and bills to pay, just like everyone else.

He told her, and her jaw almost hit the floor at what he was willing to pay for her services.

'Okay,' she heard herself reply, managing to keep her voice surprisingly steady given the circumstances. 'I'll do it. I'll need to make some arrangements with my neighbour about keeping an eye on the flat for me while I'm gone, but…well, when would you want me ready by?'

'We leave the day after tomorrow. I'll pick you up around six-thirty or seven in the morning, to beat the traffic. Pack enough for a few weeks, and don't forget to bring something waterproof. There might still be sunny skies around at the moment, but it's almost September and the region is notorious for sudden heavy showers of rain.'

Linking her hands in front of her, and feeling suddenly awkward now that the business part of their discussion was ended, Maya nodded towards the just boiled kettle.

'Right, I'll remember that. Would you like that drink I offered you now?'

Blaise glanced at his watch and she caught a tantalising glimpse of a strong-boned wrist scattered with fine dark blond hairs. Something inside her—some long-suppressed need to know the sheer physical touch of a man again *without* the attendant complications and potential deceit—was shaken dangerously awake.

'I don't think so.' The summer blue eyes locked onto hers for an instant. 'I've got various appointments I need to keep this morning, so I'd better get going. I'll see you the day after tomorrow, as arranged.'

Relief and regret pulsed through Maya at the same time. Right then she was finding it hard to stem the sense of vulnerability and need that Blaise's presence so disturbingly seemed to arouse, and because of that she definitely wanted him to leave. Yet deep in her heart some perversely opposite feeling silently protested because he wasn't going to stay longer.

'Six-thirty or seven, you said? I'll be waiting.'

She followed him to the door and down the stairs, and now it was *her* turn to study him more closely… Her skin prickled with warmth as her gaze swept the back of his tarnished gold head, the strong, masculine shoulders lovingly encased beneath the fine wool of his suit jacket, the long and no doubt hard-muscled legs negotiating the worn carpeted staircase with languorous yet athletic ease. Maya's too acute awareness was all but deluged by all she saw.

Just before opening the front door, Blaise turned back for a moment. 'I'm glad you've agreed to take the job. Where I live there's a wild beauty that if I'm away too long inevitably lures me back. Perhaps you might find it has the same effect on you, Maya?'

A flash of a strangely enigmatic smile, a turn of the head, a final glimpse of that perfect knife-edged jaw and he was gone…

There was taking risks in life and then there was knowingly setting out on a course that was hell-bent on delivering nothing but trouble… Blaise couldn't help reflecting on the latter as he expertly directed the silver Jaguar onto the long fir-tree-lined drive that led to the place he called home—a stately Jacobean dwelling nestling within towering conifers, with wisteria tumbling down its aged stone walls.

Maya had been the ideal travelling companion. She'd been perfectly amenable to conversation—*if* a little guarded—but had largely left him alone with his thoughts as he drove. Thoughts that had been inevitably consumed with *her*, did she but know it, along with constant musings on how he was going to survive the next few weeks working on his most challenging play with her distracting presence around… The woman had the *saddest* eyes Blaise had ever encountered. With the knowledge that her illustrious father had taken his own life, and having been on the receiving end of that defensive diatribe she'd launched into about men not being able to see past what she looked like, he could understand why she had such a fierce need to self-protect.

One glance into those melancholy green eyes of hers and he should have been instantly warned to steer well clear, instead of offering her a job and inviting her to stay with him in the one place where he could work in peace without intrusion. Yes, right now Blaise seemed determined to court the *worst* kind of potentially disruptive trouble as far as he was concerned…*woman* trouble. But here was the thing…regarding the gorgeous but clearly wounded Maya Hayward, he just couldn't seem to help himself…

'We're here. Welcome to Hawk's Lair.' He rolled his shoulders to ease out the stiffness accumulated there from miles of concentrated driving, then turned to smile at the slim, dark-haired woman beside him. It had been a long journey, and to be frank he was extremely relieved to have reached their destination. But instead of having his gesture reciprocated, he saw his passenger's lush pink mouth tighten worriedly, and the tension she exuded was tangible. Blaise sensed a muscle flex in his cheek.

'Struck silent, huh?' he teased, but felt an odd kind of tension of his own seizing his muscles.

'I didn't realise—' She swallowed, tucked some strands of that waterfall of black flowing hair behind her ears, and looked as though she were trying hard to compose herself.

'What?' he demanded.

'I didn't realise the house would be quite as…as grand as this,' she answered, her glance wary.

'It's a Grade One listed building, but it's still my home,' Blaise remarked matter-of-factly. 'I inherited it from my parents. You might be surprised to know that sometimes it didn't seem large *enough* when we lived there together.'

'Any particular reason why?'

'My father was apt to outbursts of quite violent temper. It just wasn't easy being around him for my mother and me.'

'I'm sorry.'

'No need to be. It's all in the past.'

Sensing the muscles in his taut stomach bunch tight at the way he'd so easily glossed over what he had been through, Blaise shrugged, silently cursing himself for being so frank…*too* frank. In future he would have to more closely guard against such off-the-cuff personal revelations.

Feeling a sudden urgent need for some fresh air, he stepped out of the car onto the gravel drive into the rapidly cooling afternoon. 'I'll get our bags out of the back,' he threw over his shoulder.

* * *

Up ahead, the front door of the house opened and a huge Irish Wolfhound bounded towards the car. It was a faintly surreal sight. In the process of making her way round to the front of the car, Maya felt her heartbeat drum painfully at the realisation that the hound was making a beeline for *her*. Remembering a childhood incident when she had been winded by the powerful bulk of an Alsatian running at her at full pelt, she froze in horror, her whole body tensing in expectation of being similarly winded again as the large dog drew nearer.

'No, Sheba! Stay!'

The forceful tone of Blaise's commanding voice cut through the mild breeze that was blowing round them and the dog came to a sudden obedient standstill, pink tongue lolling, massive head slightly bowed as it looked sheepishly towards him.

'You okay?'

It took a couple of seconds before Maya found the breath to reply. Her heart was still pounding like a hammer inside her chest. 'I'm fine... I think...'

'She was just excited to see you...weren't you, girl?'

He stooped to ruffle the hound behind the ears, and she responded by rolling on the ground in apparent ecstasy.

Maya sensed her heartbeat slowly return to normal, but she was still disturbingly emotional at the raw childhood memory that had suddenly flooded back to her. The incident had occurred at one of her father's infamous parties. The Alsatian had belonged to a world-

famous rock star that Alistair Devereaux hadn't wanted
to offend because he'd just spent a 'shed-load' of money
buying one of his paintings, and he'd made no effort
whatsoever to comfort his shocked and sobbing daughter other than to tell her to 'stop making a fuss about
nothing and go to bed'.

'All animals are basically wild and unpredictable.'
Standing tall again, Blaise was studying Maya with a
direct look that left her with nowhere to hide. 'But I'm
fairly certain Sheba wouldn't have hurt you. She was
just excited to meet someone new.'

'Why do owners of dogs always assume that those
without dogs don't mind if they jump up at them or
practically knock them down?' Maya snapped, shocked
at her own lack of control over her temper, and her
failure to keep her voice at all steady.

'There's been an incident in the past when that
happened to you? I mean when somebody's dog
knocked you down and hurt you, perhaps?'

CHAPTER FIVE

How did he guess? Was it so obvious she was scared out of her wits because a similar thing had happened before? 'Yes, a large dog did knock me down. It happened when I was about ten years old, and when it slammed into me I couldn't get my breath. I really thought I was going to die.'

'Come over here.'

'What?'

A genuine expression of concern was written on the handsome face that gazed back at her over the car bonnet, and Maya felt as though she were still that frightened ten-year-old girl, badly shaken and in need of reassurance. There was a movement to the side of her and she noticed a much older man with neatly combed silver hair dressed in navy overalls standing watching them.

'I said come over here.'

Still nervous of the Wolfhound that now lolled at Blaise's feet as though she was some playful kitten, rather than the huge, potentially *threatening* beast she actually was, Maya sucked in a shaky breath and walked forward.

'Give me your hand,' Blaise directed.

For reasons unknown to her right at that moment, she obeyed. The most delicious warmth spread through her entire being as he guided her palm gently to Sheba's head and helped her stroke it over the trimmed thick slate-grey fur that covered the dog's skull. The animal turned trusting brown eyes towards her, letting Maya know she was enjoying her touch and was not remotely hostile. Breathing was suddenly easier and she relaxed.

'See?' Blaise grinned, eyes sparkling like dazzling twin lakes shot through with sunlight as he observed her, causing a miniature firework display to be ignited in the pit of her stomach. 'She likes you. Given time, she'll become your friend and want to protect you.'

'Will I need protecting?' she quipped, her own gaze falling into his as if she was falling into the sky. He disconcerted her by saying nothing and intensifying his glance. Then, still holding onto her hand, he straightened to his full height and turned towards the elderly man in overalls.

'Come and meet Tom. He and his wife Lottie used to look after the house for my parents, and now they do the same for me.'

'Sorry about Sheba running at your lady-friend, Mr Walker,' Tom apologised, inclining his head deferentially towards Maya. 'She always knows when it's your car coming up the drive, no matter what vehicle you're driving, and I couldn't hold onto her.'

'That's okay. No harm done, I think?'

'No,' Maya agreed, smiling tentatively. To her secret disappointment, Blaise let go of her hand to clap Tom on the shoulder.

'I know she misses me when I'm away…as I miss *her*. Well, Tom, this is Maya Hayward and, as I explained to Lottie on the phone yesterday, she'll be staying at the house and working with me over the next few weeks. Is her room ready?'

'Lottie's got it all in hand, Mr Walker. But first I think she's getting a cup of tea ready for you both in the kitchen.'

'Then we'll go and find her. Will you bring our bags in? Thanks, Tom.'

The interior of the house was full of original features and beautiful artefacts, but instead of the slightly dissipated, neglected air that the various homes of her childhood had held there was a sense of grace, order and calm that had the unexpected effect of issuing a sense of calm inside Maya too.

The kitchen was large and high-ceilinged, and just as ordered as the rest of the house with its oak furniture, neat rows of blue and white porcelain on the imposing dresser and every surface gleaming with obvious care and attention. The elderly woman wearing a cheerful floral apron, who was clearly responsible for its upkeep, made no bones about displaying her pleasure at welcoming her handsome employer home again.

'There you are—and about time an' all, if you don't mind me saying so! You've been away so long I thought that all that fame and adulation in London must have gone to your head…made you forget where you really belong!' she exclaimed, and without further ado opened her arms to embrace Blaise.

'Never!' He grinned, hugging her ample frame hard. And if Maya was slightly shocked at the familiar, clearly fond way the housekeeper addressed him, she was also a little envious. To have someone waiting for you at the end of your travels to welcome you home—as if they'd been counting the days until your return—was something she had never experienced.

As Blaise stepped away from the older woman, she sensed the backs of her eyelids prickle with threatened tears. *Get a grip, Maya! What do you think you're doing? He's hired you to come and do a job for him, and he'll start to think you're some kind of emotional wreck if you carry on like this!* The familiar critic in her head that was always there to bring her back down to earth mercilessly laid into her.

'And you must be Miss Hayward?' Lottie turned her attention to Maya, warmly gripped her hand and patted it.

'Please,' the younger woman replied a little self-consciously, 'call me Maya.'

'What a beautiful name! An extremely apt one too, if you don't mind my saying so, my dear.'

'Before I show Maya to her room, we're in need of one of your excellent cups of tea, Lottie,' Blaise teased, pulling out a couple of carved oak chairs from the kitchen table and indicating with a look that Maya should sit.

'It's all ready and waiting for you, my dears. The teapot's been keeping warm for the past five minutes, and I've made some of your favourite ginger biscuits to go with it.' She bustled around, arranging plates, cups, spoons and a dainty jug of milk, and finally brought the pretty china teapot to the table, removing its clearly home-made knitted cosy to pour the tea. Then she fetched a scalloped cream plate full of the most mouth-watering and delicious-looking home-made ginger biscuits that Maya had ever seen.

'Help yourselves. I'll leave you now and go and see if Tom has brought your bags in. If you want to top up the pot, there's fresh hot water in the kettle.'

Carefully sipping her scalding hot tea, Maya relished the silence that suddenly descended. It gave her a chance to get her bearings and compose herself, even though her heart felt as if it missed a precarious beat every time she glanced across the table at Blaise.

'Your housekeeper...Lottie...she seems like a lovely lady.'

'She is. She's been mothering me since I was little. In fact, sometimes I think she forgets that I'm a grown man!'

As if *any* woman couldn't see that Blaise Walker was a man, Maya reflected, her avid glance privately examining the strongly delineated beauty in that indisputably masculine face, the stop-you-in-your-tracks blue eyes, the broad, hard-muscled shoulders beneath his casual but exquisitely tailored sports jacket.

'When did you lose your parents?' she asked, half expecting him to ignore the question. Or at the very least divert it.

'About ten years ago. Funny…it doesn't seem that long.' The azure gaze was far away for a moment. 'They were touring in Vienna with a company of local actors they'd been mentoring and the train they were travelling in derailed. They and the guard were the only fatalities.'

'I'm so sorry. So they were actors too?' Maya hadn't realised that. Was that why Blaise had initially gone into acting and not play-writing?

'Wait a minute…' The search engine inside her head whirred to a surprised stop. 'I vaguely remember hearing the news about that accident on the news… Henry and Letitia Walker were your *parents*?'

'Yes, they were.' Blaise's wary glance levelled with hers for a moment, then moved uncomfortably away again. 'Would you like some more tea?'

Again, after his surprising revelation about his father's temper, the firm reminder of his fierce need for privacy reared its head, and Maya was forced to digest the astonishing information she'd just learned in silence.

But discovering who Blaise's famous parents had been was like just learning he was the offspring of one of the high-profile glamorous couples that dominated celebrity culture today. In their time, the Walkers had commanded just as much interest and notoriety. Silently, Maya digested the fact that Blaise was also the child of famous parents.

'No. I'm fine, thanks.'

'Then have a couple of Lottie's delicious ginger biscuits. If you don't, I may just be forced to eat the whole lot myself!'

'You've got a sweet tooth, then?'

''Fraid so.'

'Blaise?'

'Yes?' Wariness made the arresting summer eyes darken—just as though a storm was coming—and Maya knew he thought she was going to question him further about his parents. He'd already indicated that his family life had had its problems, and he was probably fairly prickly about having the fact speculated on by a comparative stranger. But, knowing how she guarded her own privacy where her father was concerned, she could at least accord him the same respect.

'I won't pry into your private life, I promise. I'm here to work, and I'll try my best to do a good job for you helping with your research. You won't regret hiring me.'

'I'm sure I won't.'

His tone was brisk and all business, and Maya's throat ached with sudden unexpected hurt.

'Now, finish your tea and I'll show you where your room is. You'd probably appreciate a chance to relax then freshen up before dinner and to be frank…so would I.'

The almost companionable silence of their drive down had been replaced by a much more strained one at dinner. Stealing glances across the table at a subdued Maya, dressed in very becoming forest-green amid the flickering candlelight, somehow Blaise sensed himself become uncommunicative, on edge, and even inhabiting a state of *regret* about inviting her to come and help do the research needed for his play. Her incandescent beauty, so beguilingly captured in that incredible coveted portrait by her father when she was just fourteen, shone out no matter what she was feeling, and his painfully growing attraction for her was making a mockery of any more noble intentions he might harbour. Candidly, all Blaise could really dwell upon was his almost primal need to lose himself inside her, to feel her without censure, to experience the heat and passion he sensed lay simmering just beneath the surface of all that transparent sadness and have her incredible body join with his all night long.

With any other woman he desired the idea of becoming sexually intimate would not be nearly so complicated. But after that incident with Sheba upon their arrival at the house Blaise had again glimpsed the vulnerability and fear of being hurt in Maya's painfully truthful gaze, and setting out to deliberately seduce her would make him feel like an unscrupulous carbon copy of her detestable ex-boss. *He simply couldn't live with himself if he behaved like that.* Maya was a woman to be gently wooed and made to feel safe in a man's arms, he realised...not thoughtlessly and lustfully tangled in his sheets for a few hot nights then kissed goodbye!

Already he sensed she was the kind of girl most men probably dreamed of marrying. She had it all...beauty, intelligence, sensitivity and kindness. But, given the fine example of marital bliss he had witnessed growing up, and having seen how his father's once vigorous passion for his mother had frighteningly deteriorated into resentment, jealousy and even *violence* down the years, marriage and even a long-term relationship with a woman raised the terrifying possibility that he would turn out just like his father. *He had his genes, didn't he?* And his temper too, if he was truthful.

No...his *grande passion* was his work, and he was more than content to let that be his focus for the foreseeable future...

'Your glass is empty,' intoned the soft voice from across the table. 'Shall I pour you some more wine?'

'No, thanks.' Having been lost in the disturbing maze of his thoughts, Blaise came firmly back to the present. Unable to help himself, he let his glance sweep lazily and contemplatively across the lovely features before him, then drift down to the demure V of Maya's dress. It was a neckline that might conceal her curves far more successfully than that black velvet bombshell number he'd first seen her in, but it still paid delectable homage to enough smooth satin skin to make him want to see more.

'I've had enough. Besides…alcohol's not the answer.'

'Not the answer to what?'

'To what's bothering me right now.'

'What *is* bothering you, Blaise? I don't want to pry, but if I could help in some way…?'

Along with that soft-voiced suggestion, Maya's wide-eyed, innocent gaze sent a provocative charge of undiluted *lust* straight to Blaise's loins, leaving him aching, aroused, and frustrated as hell that he could do damn all about it right then. *Especially* when the lady who had provoked his uncomfortable condition seemed completely oblivious to his dilemma!

'Blaise?' she prompted, sounding concerned.

'It's nothing to worry about. I was only thinking about the play and how much there is to do. Tomorrow I need to crack on with it, and in order to do that my mind needs to be clear and sharp. What I'm saying is that I think I'll call it a day. Hope you don't mind? I'll see you in the morning, Maya. Sleep well.'

And with this sudden declaration he pushed to his feet, dropped his napkin on the table next to the polished candelabra with its soft flickering candlelight, then swiftly exited the room. No doubt leaving his beautiful new assistant to perplexedly ponder at her leisure on his sudden and rather abrupt need to leave…

The next morning, as he walked into the kitchen craving his usual cup of strong black coffee, the frustration of the previous night had scarcely improved. Even a hot, invigorating shower had failed to banish either the sensuous aching that had seized his body *or* the thoughts in his head that seemed obsessed with just one thing and one thing alone…*making love to Maya.*

A relentless tide of lust and desire for her had mercilessly tormented Blaise all night, keeping him awake practically from midnight to dawn. Only when the softly smudged pinkish-grey light of morning had streamed through the bedroom windows—windows that he invariably left uncovered and opened in the summer—had he perversely managed to close his eyes and fall into a deep sleep.

'Good morning.'

The reason for his disturbed night stood in front of him, stirring a mug of coffee at the kitchen counter. She was dressed in fitted black jeans that hugged hips and thighs goddess-like enough to send every male from here to Alaska howling in delight at the sight of her and thanking the universe that he'd been born a man. On her top half she wore another fitted white cotton shirt that couldn't help but make much of the fact that her waist was *tiny* and her bust was… Well, he couldn't think of a single epithet just then that would do it justice. All Blaise could do instead was recall the sight of it contained in that knock-out black dress he'd first seen her in, and he was turned on all over again…*instantly*. To complete the highly arresting package she made, a small carved butterfly on a fine gold chain nestled at the base of her smooth skinned throat, and her emerald eyes gazed back at him like those of one who had slept the sleep of the innocent and woken as refreshed and rested as it was possible to be.

Because Blaise felt so grouchy, it was a double kick in the guts to encounter her fresh-faced loveliness and know that in comparison he must look like a man who had just crept out of some God-forsaken cave in the desert, where he'd slept on rocks all night!

'Good morning.' His voice sounded as if he'd been gargling with rusty nails too. 'Sleep well?'

'It's the best night's sleep I've had in years! Honestly, I'm not joking. The sofa-bed I use at home is hardly the most comfortable thing in the world, and I usually wake up in the morning aching all over and feeling like I've been kicked by a donkey!'

'Doesn't sound very appealing, I have to say.'

'Trust me…it's not. Would you like some coffee? Lottie had the percolator going when I came in and told me to help myself.'

'Please.'

'And how about some breakfast? I told Lottie I could see to it, as she'd got a pile of ironing to be getting on with.'

'Not for me, thanks, but you go ahead if you want something.'

'I'm fine. I never eat much in the mornings…so just some coffee for you, then?'

'That's all, thanks.'

He sat down at the table, scraped both hands backwards and forwards through his already tousled hair, and tried to force his distracted mind to focus on the play. In the entire history of his writing career never had anything been more seriously difficult…if not downright *impossible*…as he watched Maya cheerfully pour his coffee and bring it across to him, his gaze fixated on the gentle sway of those womanly hips in her spectacularly well-fitting jeans.

'I'm really looking forward to starting work today,' she enthused, gracefully dropping down into the oak chair opposite.

'Are you?' Sarcasm scarcely cloaked the frustration in Blaise's tone 'Well, if you're feeling so full of get up and go perhaps you'd care to write the play *for* me?'

'Is something wrong?'

A fleeting shadow of hurt passed across the vividly crystal irises and Blaise silently cursed himself. 'I had a rough night, that's all. And before you say it…I'm *begging* you…please don't ask if there's anything you can do to help!'

CHAPTER SIX

HIS gaze was hot, focused, and *definitely* aroused. Suddenly Maya knew very well why he had warned her not to offer to help. He had worn that same drowsy lustful 'I could eat you up' glance when he'd looked at her last night at dinner…just before he had declared that alcohol wasn't the answer to whatever was bothering him.

But last night she had somehow fooled herself about what should have been as plain as the nose on her face. Before Blaise had offered her this job he had made it more than clear that he wanted to see her again, that he was attracted to her. Now Maya could no longer hide from the fact that he *wanted* her. The idea caused a lava flow of heat to erupt inside, making her squeeze her thighs together and squirm in her seat. Her body *definitely* responded to the libidinous signals Blaise was giving her, and indeed *echoed* them—yet because of her devastating past *acting* on her feelings was a frightening leap she just wasn't ready to contemplate. Especially when she already knew that it had no future in it.

'Is this going to get in the way of us working together?' she asked quietly, staring down at the table. She continued, 'Because I really want the chance to show you…to prove that I'm a fast learner where learning new skills is concerned and that I can be a genuine asset to you.'

'*Nothing* gets in the way of my writing… Just because I'm attracted to you it doesn't mean I'm going to throw the baby out with the bathwater! I still have a play to write.' The broad shoulders lifted in a tense little shrug that couldn't help but reveal his frustration. 'And I still need someone to do my research. As far as I'm concerned, you've got every chance of proving you can do a good job, Maya.'

'Good.' She relaxed.

'But sex *can* be recreational too, you know.'

His words swept through her like a violent tornado.

'For you maybe…but not for me'

'Is that because you got hurt by someone, or just because you're holding out for something more serious?'

'Won't you talk to me about the play?' Taking a swift sip of her rapidly cooling coffee, Maya prayed her question was diverting enough to steer Blaise away from the far more *dangerous* ground he was currently intent on travelling…

Drumming his fingers on the table, he let a knowing little smile touch his lips 'Because it's safer?'

'Probably… But I do really want to know what you're writing about and hear your suggestions on what I need to research first.'

Sheba chose that very moment to pad into the kitchen and glance hopefully at them both. Studying the Wolfhound with far less wariness than she had yesterday, Maya smiled.

'It must be just like having a small horse in the house, having Sheba about the place!'

'Something like that,' Blaise agreed, beckoning the animal to him and ruffling her fondly behind the ears. The dog sat, happily allowing him to make the fuss she'd obviously been seeking and clearly adoring him.

'I suppose we ought to take her for a walk before starting work.' He glanced across at Maya, his gaze friendly and with no hint of tension in those superlative blue eyes at all.

'You want me to come too?'

'Good opportunity to show you some of the country-side and talk about the play at the same time,' he answered, rising to his feet with Sheba swiftly following suit…

Hadrian's Wall was between seventy-six and eighty miles long, she'd learned. For the past two hours Maya and Blaise had negotiated merely four miles of it, with Sheba bounding along in front of them. Built on high ground, it had been a fairly steep climb. But Maya loved walking over the uneven crags alongside the wall, seeing the lichen scattered between the rocks, and clumps of gorse and purple-flowered comfrey wherever they glanced, climbing uphill one minute and then downhill the next, with the wind in her hair and the heady fragrance of genuinely unpolluted, clean fresh air in her lungs.

Blaise threw her an enquiring look as they moved steadily uphill again, clearly noticing that her breath came a little quicker at the exertion. Below them was a glorious panorama of the most wonderful countryside Maya had ever seen, consisting of clumps of ancient trees, verdant fields and tarns, sparkling rivers glinting in the midday sunlight, and every so often she simply had to stop and take stock of what she was seeing. To drink it in and count her blessings that she was privileged enough to be there, enjoying it.

'How are you holding up? It can be quite a climb in places.'

'I'm doing fine. It's challenging, because I'm a little bit out of shape at the moment, but I honestly love it,' Maya replied, emerald eyes shining.

'I would never have called you out of shape, Maya.' His tone huskily wry, Blaise let his glance deliberately track up and down her body for a moment. Heat invaded her.

'I mean I'm probably quite unfit. Living in London, I just don't get the exercise that I'd probably be motivated to get out here, where I can breathe in all this wonderful fresh air instead of traffic fumes. You're so lucky living in such an amazing place.'

She could hear her heart pounding in her ears, and frantically hunted for a way to keep the conversation neutral.

'You said that the main character in your play is a young Roman soldier responsible for helping guard and patrol some of the sentry posts along the wall?'

'That's right.'

'Where did he come from? Rome?'

'No. The soldiers came mainly from a place in Belgium—known in ancient times as Tungria.'

'Oh? Can you tell me a bit more about what happens to him?'

He had told her a little of the story, and what he needed her to research, and right from the start Maya had been intrigued by it. It was the heartbreaking tale of a young boy in Roman times—a boy with a head full of dreams of glory, running away from home and his family's farm to join the Roman army—who, when he got to Britannia, met a local girl from one of the settlements and fell in love. The soldiers then had been forbidden to marry, and their liaison had to be conducted in secret.

'Well…' Blaise gazed out into the middle distance for a couple of moments, considering Maya's question. 'Eventually the soldier is killed, during a night attack on the wall, but before he dies he finds out that his sweetheart is pregnant with his child, and he vows to find a way for them to return to his village so that they can marry. Frankly, he is tired of being a soldier—killing men in skirmishes and attacks to preserve land for a conquering army—and has become increasingly disenchanted with his role. He soberly reflects on the benefits of a simple rural life, raising a family and earning a living from what he can grow on his land.'

He continued thoughtfully, 'Yes, we can travel all round the world in pursuit of our dreams, only to realise the treasure we were so avidly in search of is already right here in front of us.' He jerked his head towards the stunning vista surrounding them. 'The taking of a life is a dreadful thing, and violence can never be the answer,' he added, sighing, 'however much we seek to justify it. First we need to examine the violence in ourselves, I think. Ultimately, that's what the play is about.'

As he'd been speaking, a gust of strong wind had torn through the tousled dark gold lock of hair that flopped onto his brow, and Maya stared transfixed at the chiselled beauty of features that were suddenly thrown into stark and breathtaking relief. She was utterly fascinated that to highlight the theme he'd chosen—and he was writing a play about youthful dreams turning into a nightmare—he had used *a story about love*…

Before she realised it, she heard herself ask, 'What were your own dreams as a boy?'

On the brow of that windblown hill, Blaise studied Maya for what felt like an eternity before replying. When he did eventually answer her question, his voice sounded calm and steady. 'To express myself creatively in the way that I chose and be good at it…and funnily enough to be happy.'

'And *are* you happy?'

'Are you?'

'That's not fair!' Maya protested, taken aback at how easily he'd turned the tables on her.

'Then answer me this instead… What were *your* dreams as a young girl?'

Knowing that he was definitely issuing her with a challenge, Maya dug her hands into the pockets of her denim jacket and wondered what to tell him. In the end, because the penetrating beam of his gaze left her with no hiding place, she elected to be honest.

'To grow up, find someone I wanted to be with for ever—someone who really loved me—and have a family. I was never ambitious for a big career or wealth or anything like that. But…' she dipped her head and stared at the ground '…it was a childish dream. Now that I'm grown up I'm fully aware just how difficult such a deceptively simple dream is to achieve, and I just take one day at a time and try to enjoy what I *have* got.'

'What about artistic talent? You didn't inherit any desire to maybe do what your father did?'

'No…I didn't. I can't draw or paint to save my life. Are you disappointed?'

Feeling a sickening sensation of genuine hurt well up inside her in case he was, Maya turned away from the lancing gaze that so easily took her apart and started walking down the hill again, her heart still hammering as her booted feet carefully negotiated the uneven crags that covered the ground.

Sensing a flash of something beside her, she glanced down at a panting Sheba, the large noble head held ever so slightly at an angle as she came to a halt, just as if she was asking her what was the matter and could she help? The thought was so preposterous that she found herself smiling. Reaching out, Maya gently stroked her hand over the slate-grey fur that covered the dog's extensive back without any fear whatsoever.

'It's all right, Sheba. I'm fine...honest.'

Asking her if she'd had any desire to follow in her father's footsteps had obviously been too close to the bone and Blaise should have known better. Especially when he had fielded many similar questions himself over the years, because of his own famous parentage. Yet somehow an increasing desire to get Maya to open up to him, to make a real connection with her, had unexpectedly manifested itself inside him. He'd never experienced such a powerful need around a woman before and, startled, he let the idea wash over him, feeling what it was like. Her confession that her one-time dream had been to be with someone who really loved her and to have a family had also perversely made him want to instantly back away…to maintain the emotional distance that he realised both of them subconsciously fought hard for.

Contemplating her now as she stroked Sheba, the gusting wind turning her long flowing hair into a riotous cloud of ebony silk, Blaise remembered the upsetting memory she'd revealed about being winded by a similarly powerful dog when she was small, and the fact that she'd taken the courageous step of petting the animal in front of him with such apparent ease filled him with honest admiration for her sheer gutsiness.

'Let's press on, shall we?' he called out, lest any more warm feelings of admiration take precedence over the play he was meant to be thinking about. 'We've got a lot to do today.'

Deftly negotiating the jagged crags that separated them down the hill, Blaise arrived beside the stunning brunette and the Wolfhound in next to no time, and with not even the merest hint of being out of breath added, 'Lottie will have lunch prepared in another hour. And she's a stickler for timekeeping when it comes to meals at Hawk's Lair.'

'That's such an evocative name. Where did it come from?' Maya asked, and he saw the telltale smudges of what he suspected was the residue of tears beneath her emerald eyes.

For a moment his heart squeezed with regret, and he had to fight the strongest urge to wipe them away.

'My father started out in a local repertory company

in the small Scottish town where he came from and once performed in a play that had the title.' Blaise shrugged. 'My mother had seen him in it and thought the name so romantic that when they bought the house here, she insisted on calling it Hawk's Lair.'

'And was it a romantic play?'

'No…it most definitely wasn't! It was a stinging satire about a corrupt politician.'

'Still,' Maya said quickly, but not quickly enough to hide her apparent disappointment, 'it's a great name.'

'Maya?'

'Yes?'

'It was crass of me to ask if you had any ambition to be like your father.' He lifted her chin and cupped her small perfect jaw in the cradle of his hand. 'Do you forgive me?'

'Of course.' But she moved quickly away as she said it, turning only briefly back to enquire, 'That sycamore tree you mentioned earlier that's supposed to be a famous landmark… How far did you say it was from here?'

Fuelled by her challenging walk to see the famous Roman wall, along with Lottie's excellent lunch of grilled fresh salmon, new potatoes and a warm salad, Maya was just as eager as Blaise to start work.

During lunch he had expanded a little bit more on the play, and just what he was looking for research-wise, and as they'd talked she'd become more and more transfixed by the animation she heard in his mellifluous voice. Animation that she also witnessed etched in the sublime contours of his handsome face. It was a master-class in inspiration, and by the end of it Maya fervently wished that she had some up until now undiscovered talent so that she could help him move forward with what she'd learned.

After lunch they made a brief detour to the extensive library on the floor upstairs, where Blaise informed her she could find just about every history book she'd need, then came back downstairs to his huge study. He showed Maya into the smaller connecting office, where she was set up with a computer, use of the internet, printer, scanner, and a small but extensive bookshelf crammed with books in which to search for information.

'I've asked Lottie to make dinner for eight tonight instead of seven…do you mind? I'd like to work on as long as possible before we break again.' Standing by the door leading back into his study, Blaise briefly checked his watch before settling his arresting gaze once again on Maya.

She almost had to shake herself out of the trance she'd fallen into. That voice of his was a seductive weapon, bent on the complete capitulation of the listener, she was certain. Along with the sheer sensual heat that radiated from his hard, leanly muscular body, it made her knees almost buckle and every muscle she possessed contract with an answering devastating warmth.

'I—I hope you don't think this sounds too weird…' to cover her confusion she started to babble '…but when we were out there walking alongside the wall, I could almost hear the marching feet of the Roman soldiers—as though…as though the sound was contained and preserved in the very earth… Do you know what I mean?'

What she told him was absolutely true, but the way Blaise was studying her made Maya feel as if he'd just moved his body right up next to hers and demanded she kiss him. His pupils had contracted with genuine surprise at what she'd said.

'I do know what you mean. I've had the same thought myself many times when I was up there. The place is full of ghosts from the past. You're obviously very sensitive and receptive to that sort of thing.'

Ghosts from the past… Maya shuddered softly. She certainly knew about those. 'Well, I'll let you get on. I'm fine with dinner at eight.'

'Good.' Delaying his departure by another couple of disconcerting seconds as his glance lazily drifted across her face, Blaise finally moved away back into his own office and closed the door behind him.

Maya had returned to her room to change for dinner. Having showered and got ready in double-quick time himself, Blaise sat on the edge of the huge king-sized bed he occupied alone and tried to think over the progress he'd made on the play.

Trouble was...every time he tried to focus on the day's work the TV screen of his mind kept switching to the channel where Maya had the starring role. Too restless to patiently sit and wait for her, he got up and went out into a corridor lined with much of the highly covetable art both he and his parents had collected over the years. Maya's room was about halfway down the corridor from his and, scrubbing his hand round his newly shaven jaw, Blaise rapped smartly on the oak panelling. Half hoping she'd answer the door wrapped in just a towel, or that short little robe she'd had on that morning he'd called on her unexpectedly in Camden, he felt his lips twitch with a wry grin. He was behaving like a schoolboy who had just hit puberty with a vengeance! But then this was one bewitchingly beautiful woman, and when he was around her it just didn't seem possible for him to behave like anything else.

She wasn't just beautiful either...she was intelligent and sensitive too. Not to mention *damaged* by whatever had gone on in her past. The grin on his lips vanished as he soberly considered if he wouldn't live to regret inviting her to work for him after all.

'Hi. Am I taking too long? Just let me put my shoes on.'

Fragrant and bare-footed, Maya greeted him at the door, her long dark hair flowing down over the black silk sleeveless top she wore with matching palazzo-style trousers, dazzling green eyes bright as newly polished crystal. Blaise took one look at her and knew he had never wanted anything in his life *more...*

CHAPTER SEVEN

'THERE'S no hurry. I just thought we'd go down to dinner together. Go put your shoes on…take your time. I'll wait.'

'Why don't you come in, then?' Her skin flushed a little as she said this, and Blaise saw with satisfaction that she was equally as affected by seeing him as he was her.

Accepting her invitation, he entered the room and shut the door behind him. Hurrying across to the wardrobe to retrieve a pair of flat gold sandals, Maya sat back on the bed to put them on, inadvertently giving him a highly arousing glimpse of her scarlet-painted toenails. But then out of the corner of his eye he saw the portrait of her as a child propped up against a striped slipper chair, and a jolt of surprise shot through him.

'You brought the picture.' Drawn by its beauty, as he had been before, he found himself standing in front of it, all the better to study it more closely.

'I always take it with me on longer trips.' A rustle of

silk, the scent of some sweetly floral perfume, and its owner suddenly stood there beside him.

'Presumably you have it well insured?'

As soon as the words were out of his mouth Blaise sensed the abrupt shift in Maya's mood. Crossing her arms over her chest, she turned her head to glare at him.

'I don't care about its monetary value!' she exclaimed passionately. 'Do you think that means anything to me?'

'Then what *does* it mean to you, Maya?' he asked gently.

Moving back towards the bed, she collected the cream pashmina she'd left lying there. 'It's a piece of my father. The piece he couldn't give to me when he was alive.'

Seeing her wrestle with whatever powerful emotion was flowing through her, Blaise judged it best not to speak right then. Instead he moved across the room to join her…*waiting*.

'You see…he was always busy working, or—or partying with his celebrity friends, and he didn't always have much time for me. That day—the day he started work on the portrait—he was more like the father I'd dreamed of him being. And although I was grumpy, because he rarely ever gave me much attention and I barely knew how to handle it when he did, I secretly loved him doing that portrait of me. That's why I wouldn't sell it…no matter how much it's worth.'

'And that's all he left you after he died? His career was amazing. He must have had other assets, surely?'

'What assets? Everything he had was either sold to help pay off his debts or given away to some—some sycophant whilst he was intoxicated! We even lost our house… But he'd died before that happened, and it couldn't have mattered less to me that everything material had gone.'

Suddenly understanding why she lived in a poky studio flat, with not much evidence of anything of material value, Blaise took the soft pashmina out of Maya's hands, threw it back on the bed, then placed his hands either side of her waist. It was slender as a reed—no more than a man's hand span—and he easily sensed the heat from her body through the silky material of her blouse.

'What was he like as a man…your father? Will you tell me about him?'

Clearly startled by the question, Maya momentarily withdrew her gaze, as if to regroup her thoughts, but to his satisfaction did not move out of the circle of intimacy he'd instigated.

'Like many artistic people he was very complex…brilliant and *driven*, but easily led too. His weakness was anything addictive—anything that was ultimately bad for him. When he lost my mother he lost a little of his grip on reality, I think. He tried to take care of me in his own muddled fashion, but he really wasn't the type of man who could cope with children. He just didn't have a clue what I needed. Often he left me on my own for long periods. At one time we lived in a house a bit similar to this, and I can remember at nights huddling in a corner of my bedroom terrified of every sound, every creak of a floorboard or tree branch moving in the wind, convinced someone was going to break in and either kill me or…or take me away.'

The long, tremulous sigh she released feathered over him, and Blaise realised that his heart was pounding like a sledgehammer in his chest at what she'd told him. Now a couple of the disparaging references she'd made to fame started to make sense. *What had Devereaux been thinking of, leaving his young daughter to fend for herself?* Surely the neglect of a child was one of the most despicable cruelties of all? The man had obviously been too wrapped up in chasing his desires and addictions to tend to his daughter's welfare, and in Blaise's book that was pretty damn unforgivable.

'No wonder you were frightened.' There was a slight break in his voice as his hand lifted to brush away some soft dark hair that had drifted across her cheekbone. 'You had a right to be. You were just a child, Maya.'

Her lip visibly trembled. Then her stunning eyes filled with tears. 'Don't do that!'

'Do what?'

'Be so understanding and…and say nice things to me. Kindness is the hardest thing to cope with of all. Better that you just tell me to forget about the past and concentrate on the present. Isn't that what people say?' Anguished, her beautiful emerald gaze latched a little desperately onto his. 'Trouble is…sometimes I *can't* forget about the past. I feel like I'm still waiting for him to come back, you know? Still waiting for him to walk through that door and say all the things I longed for him to say to me when I was a little girl…most of all to tell me that everything would be all right…even if it was a lie. But of course he won't come back, will he? He even took his own life to get away from me!'

'Is that what you believe? My God, Maya, that's got to be a million miles from the truth!'

'Is it? How do you know?'

'Because people aren't in their right minds when they take their own life. They're so locked in their pain that they can't see any other way of escaping it. That's the only reason they would make such a dreadful decision. It's nobody's *fault*, and you definitely shouldn't be blaming yourself for what happened. I also know that you absolutely deserve people to be kind to you…to treat you well. Your father was ill and needed help. Maybe right now what *you* need is a little help and kindness too?'

'That's where you're wrong. People's help or kindness usually comes with a price attached, I've found. Frankly I'd rather fend for myself.' She tried to twist away from him, but Blaise held her fast, forcing her to look at him.

'I don't believe you.'

In a heartbeat, his lips were on hers. No thinking, no planning, no intent to seduce… He merely acted on pure primal *instinct* and a genuine need to provide solace to the woman in his arms in whatever way he could. But once he'd laid his lips against hers, and her mouth had opened to him as easily and effortlessly as a flower opening its petals to the sun, a fire caught hold of him—a rampaging torrent of want, need and desire that was like a forceful, unstoppable river…

His arms wound tightly about her, Blaise was kissing her as if he was drunk on the taste of her and it was utterly *blissful*. Just as Maya had always guessed it would be. She had no reservations about kissing him back either. In a state of heightened emotion already, she knew her blood was pounding with the kind of carnal heat that she'd read about in books and passionate poetry but had no personal experience of. Her hands moved urgently down over his hard, fit body, pushing at the black fine wool sweater he wore, touching the warm, taut flesh of his ribcage and stomach underneath, aching to explore even more of him.

He too was impatient with her clothing, and he lifted the silky top that clung to her body, moving the sensuous material urgently up over her lacy black bra, kneading her breasts through the flimsy cups, teasing her burgeoning nipples with rough, warm fingers and making her want to plead with him for more of the same exquisite treatment with no end in sight.

When his hands travelled down to her hips, to impel

her hard against him, she came into contact with the full dizzying strength of his desire. It strained hard against the fly of his jeans and left Maya in no doubt that he was as turned on as she was. With a hungry little groan she moulded his taut firm behind through the black denim he had on, a sudden wild need driving her to have him possess her...*now*. She didn't want to wait. The desperate demand of her body to have him void the ache inside her in the most primeval way was too great for either conscience or patience to play any part in at all, yet somewhere in her mind she knew it was danger-ously crazy as well.

But gradually, bit by devastating bit, Blaise made the decision to call a halt to the madness and broke off their passionate kiss. He lifted his head to study her. His blue eyes reflected back a hot, restless sea of need and desire that easily matched her own as they ruefully met hers.

'Lottie is expecting us down for dinner, and I can't do anything to delay that right now, but I don't want to leave you in a state of wanting either. Why don't you lie on the bed for me?'

Dazed by his mellifluous voice and that tantalising instruction, Maya tugged her top back down over her bra. 'What—what for?'

'Maya...do you really need to ask?'

Eyeing him nervously, Maya found herself doing as he'd asked her—just as if her body made its own deci-sions without even consulting her mind. Turning her head, she watched him move across to the lamp beside her bed like a fluid ebony shadow—the only relief his dark gold hair—and switch it on. Then he flicked another switch and the main light went off. Her very ribs aching with the tension that was building inside her, she forced herself to try and relax even as the room was bathed in a soft, intimate glow.

Returning, Blaise slipped off her shoes—and even the touch of his hands at her bare ankles sent hot darts of torrid pleasure bolting almost violently through her. Then, crouching down by the bed in front of her, he eased her long legs towards him. In another fluid, commanding motion he moved upwards to undo her zip, tugging her black silk trousers down over her hips and legs in a rustle of sensuous silk before discarding them onto the bed.

Her breath catching in her throat, Maya leaned forward to see what he would do next. Never had her heart beat with such clamouring, urgent need—and it had to be said *fear* too. This was simply out of her remit. To be so vulnerable with a man again was like cracking open a fissure in her heart that had not yet healed. It would all end in tears…she knew that. But it was with devastating intent that Blaise met and held her enraptured gaze. In response, her skin prickled hotly, as though a thousand tropical winds were blowing over her and through her. She was hardly conscious of breathing as he hooked his thumbs beneath the black lace sides of her panties and then, with a firm downward tug, deftly removed them too.

Biting her lip, she lay back on the bed, her body trembling so hard that she physically hurt. With the tight, coiled feeling inside her hitting an impossible ceiling, she knew she was on the brink of climaxing already because of Blaise's sensual attentions.

It wouldn't take much to tip her over the edge, she realised.

'Try to relax…trust me. I'm going to give you just what you need…I promise…' His voice flowed over her like warm, luscious honey in the most seductively hypnotic tone she'd ever heard.

Telling herself she was only fulfilling a very basic need—a need she'd long denied herself with a man— Maya shut her eyes. Almost instantly she opened them again. Shock and dizzying hot pleasure poured through her in a volcanic rush as his velvet tongue laved at the soft exquisitely sensitive folds at her centre, across the aching bud there, and then thrust commandingly inside her.

Maya hardly knew how she stayed on the bed the pleasure was so intense. All she could do was gasp and moan out loud, her fingers clutching desperately for purchase into the luxurious silk counterpane, her body helplessly writhing as Blaise's thrusts became more and more purposeful. And then she couldn't hold back any longer. An ecstatic cry left her throat as she convulsed with the power of her climax, and still he tormented and thrilled her with that erotic tongue of his—holding her slender thighs firmly apart until she writhed and convulsed no more.

All but exhausted by the ecstatic release he had helped her attain, Maya slowly returned to the world and dazedly sat up. Quite aware of how wild and wanton she must appear, with her long hair falling in a tousled silken mass round her shoulders and the lower half of her body bare and exposed, she self-consciously drew her knees together, feeling her sense of vulnerability magnify. It was the most vulnerable and exposed she had ever felt with a man, and her anxiety at what she'd dared let him do flowed over her, almost stealing every bit of the wild, unfettered pleasure she'd just enjoyed.

If she knew herself to appear wanton, then Blaise looked downright *lascivious* as he got to his feet. Leaning over her, he tilted her face towards him and delivered a most *knowing* masculine grin.

'That was just for starters,' he teased, then gently moved the pads of his fingers downwards over her cheeks, where the damp trails of her tears still glistened. 'I wanted to help you forget the past and come back to the present.'

'You—you certainly did that.' One corner of her mouth somehow quirked upwards in a smile that, given what she'd just allowed him to do, was ridiculously shy.

'We'll continue where we left off later. I want you

in my bed tonight, Maya… In fact the truth is I want you anywhere I can have you.'

Without hesitation she touched his smoothly shaven jaw, forcing her anxiety away and for once bravely meeting the burning gaze that surveyed her without withdrawing, 'I want that too,' she answered softly, and this time it was Blaise's audible intake of breath that feathered over her…

Neither of them was able to do full justice to the beautiful dinner Lottie had prepared. *Not when a different sort of hunger was gnawing at them instead.* With the candlelight glowing between them on the polished dining table, even conversation seemed extraneous. When Blaise asked her to pass him one of the condiments in its antique silver container Maya reacted just as if he'd just asked her to peel off her clothes and lie naked on the table. Her skin *burned* where his fingers inadvertently brushed against hers, and when she glanced up into his eyes he was studying her so fervently that her breath was suspended for a couple of moments.

'What is it?' she whispered.

'I want to know how long it's been since you've been with someone,' he replied.

'I haven't been with anybody for at least two years.' Troubled, she blushed hard at the idea that he might believe her to be promiscuous in any way. After all, she'd just allowed him the most intimate access to her body—*more* intimate than she'd ever let any other man come *close* to getting.

'Was it a long relationship?'

Thinking about Sean Rivers was not something Maya liked to do very often. Even now she shuddered at how bitterly their liaison had ended. 'It lasted about six months, so...not very long at all.'

'Why did it end?'

'Because I trusted him a bit too much and he threw my trust right back in my face.'

'Oh?'

'Something happened.' She took a small sip of wine, the alcohol bolstering her courage. 'His name was Sean, and for a while I thought I was in love with him...thought that he loved me too. He was the first man I'd ever met who made me think our relationship could go some-where. When we were together he—he was tender, kind, caring. We'd talk and talk for hours, on every subject under the sun...even about becoming engaged.'

Maya's glance was far away for a moment as memories of that liaison came flooding back. 'He was all the things I thought I'd ever wanted in a man. Then one day I received a text from him...an intimate, private message—the sort of thing that a man sends to the woman he loves. Only it wasn't for me...he'd sent it to me accidentally. That was the day I discovered he was having an affair with somebody else.'

Swallowing hard at the aching memory of yet again

being betrayed by someone she'd trusted, Maya reached up to curl a few silken black strands of hair behind her ear. 'My friends said I should have seen the signs. But people also say that love makes you blind, don't they? Anyway, I didn't see them—the signs, I mean. I stupidly believed everything he said and I paid for it. I rang him straight away and told him I never wanted to see him again. I *didn't*. Clearly the other woman meant much more to him than I did.'

'That's tough. I'm sorry you had to find out the truth in such a crass way,' Blaise commented thoughtfully, slowly twisting the stem of his crystal wine glass between long fingers as he regarded her. 'But better that you found out his true character sooner rather than later.'

'And what about you as far as relationships are concerned?' Maya dared, watching how the candlelight cast some of his amazing sculpted features into shadow and the others into mesmerising relief—including the sexy little dimple that cleaved into his chin. Sensing that guard of his descend almost immediately, she half expected him not to tell her, and she couldn't help but feel a little crushed that he would withhold such information after what she'd just revealed about her ex.

A sickening fear arose inside that he would turn out to be some kind of international playboy, with a woman in every port, and that he would break her heart. *But what if she could steel her heart against full-blooded involvement with Blaise?* What if she could accept a short-term affair instead? An affair with no expectations on her part other than more of the scalding passion she had enjoyed earlier? What then?

'My most enduring relationship has always been with my work,' he answered, with not a small touch of his trademark irony in his tone. Before continuing he drained the rest of the shimmering ruby wine in his glass. 'I've always adored women...but as yet I've never found one I wanted to spend the rest of my life with.'

'Did you even *want* to?' Maya questioned unhappily, suddenly knowing that, for Blaise, the notion of happy ever after with a woman he adored was probably not even on the agenda, if the truth be known. Now she considered again the possibility that he was one of those men who liked to play the field, to have his cake and eat it, as the old saying went.

And why wouldn't he when he moved in the kind of circles where beautiful available women must be ten a penny? The small corner of Maya's heart that had started to blossom beneath his kind words and sexy attention started to close up again—like a flower denied sunlight—and the sensation of an icy breeze rippled through her instead...even though she'd already tried to resign herself to a brief affair with him.

Sensing the downturn in her mood, Blaise smiled coaxingly at her. 'Come on, Maya. Let's not spoil this thing we have between us already.' Frustration edged his tone.

'Oh?' she pushed to her feet, too upset to stay sitting. 'And what is this "thing" we have between us, exactly… *recreational sex*? Of course…how could I forget?'

CHAPTER EIGHT

SHE'D left the table before Blaise could fully register the fact.

'Damn!' What had he said to make her act so unreasonably? He didn't like the way he was suddenly feeling: as if *he* were one of those despicable men that had jerked her around—and he included her tragic father in that list. He'd been perfectly up-front from the start, hadn't he? Even though he'd offered her the job as his temporary research assistant he'd made it crystal-clear that he desired her too, so what was she getting upset about? Covering his face with his hands, Blaise swore softly.

Minutes later, he found himself standing outside Maya's bedroom for the second time that evening. As he rapped on the door, he was genuinely shocked at what a heightened state of emotion he was in. Not since he was a child, witnessing that first terrible row where his father had hit his mother across the face, had he felt so affected. God! What was the matter with him? He'd become expert over the years at disguising his feelings, and sometimes wondered if he hadn't done *too* good a job. Most of the women he'd had relationships with had all but *despaired* that he was even capable of experiencing emotion, yet here he was, turned every which way imaginable because of the woman whose room he now waited outside.

'I'm sorry I stormed off like that.' The door opened and there she stood.

'I somehow think maybe I owe you an apology too.' But even as the words left Blaise's lips confusion bolted through him…confusion *and* arousal. Dressed only in a short striped nightshirt, her feet and long legs bare and the neckline of the shirt opened provocatively low enough for him to easily glimpse the sexy, tantalising curve of those voluptuous breasts, Maya stared steadily back at him. His reaction was inevitable. He hardened instantly, as though a searing torch of flaming heat had glanced against his loins.

'What's all this about?' he asked huskily, marvelling that he was able to speak at all when he was confronted by what was probably the most alluring sight even *his* fertile imagination could devise.

'I thought you were meant to be clever? You write all these amazing plays about the human condition, and you can't work out why I'm standing here dressed like this? I've been waiting for you, Blaise. If you want to have an affair with me then I've decided that's exactly what I want too. I promise you I'll have no expectations other than that.'

'Is that right?'

'Yes. It's what you wanted, isn't it? After all…we're both grown-ups here, aren't we?'

Her cheeks turned visibly pink as she made this declaration but, gazing into her hypnotic dark-lashed emerald eyes, Blaise could see that though a part of her might be mad at him for clearly not wanting anything more than an affair with her she was still equally as aroused as he was. Stepping over the threshold into the room, the intimate space lit only by that same diaphanous glow that had lit it earlier, he knew his hungry glance devoured her. Devoured her like no tempting dessert he'd ever sampled.

Taking a long, slow breath, he remarked carefully, 'Never mind what *I* want. I'm moving no further from this spot unless I know for sure that this is absolutely what you want too, Maya.'

'It is. It *is* what I want. I've told you already, haven't I?'

'You're sure?' He raised her chin to bring her revealing ardent glance level with his,

'Yes…yes!' she cried. 'Of *course* this is what I want! What do I have to do to prove it to you? I've tried going for love and it turned out to be far too painful for me to ever want it again. An affair is all I'm looking for, Blaise.'

'Okay. You've convinced me.' Now Blaise's hand moved to the open V of her nightshirt, and in a heart-beat he tore it down the centre, causing the tiny white buttons to fly in all directions. Pushing the gaping material aside, he let his gaze feast on Maya's beauti-ful breasts, with their perfectly *edible* café mocha tips, before ravenous need drove him to sample each one in turn, suckling, tasting and wetting them with the heat and moisture from his swirling, greedy tongue.

Her fingers were in his hair, urging him on, and Blaise slid his hands between her legs and pushed into her with his fingers. Her damp heat engulfed him, and her slender body quivered and sagged against him as a long, low moan left her throat.

Tugging his sweater over his head and unfastening his jeans, he yanked Maya roughly against him, branding her mouth with a hot, sexy kiss that was *beyond* hungry, beyond any carnal craving he'd ever ex-perienced before, as basic and animal as a kiss could be and with no pretence of gentleness whatsoever. *Not even a drop.* At one point Blaise even tasted blood on his lips, and couldn't be sure whether it was his or Maya's. All he knew was that a storm was building between them—a storm whose only way of stopping was to burn itself out. *Well, he was burning.* So burning hot and turned on that he thought he might lose his mind if he didn't take her soon.

Even as the erotic realisation filled him, electrifying

his body to the exclusion of everything else, he was dragging Maya down to the luxuriously carpeted floor, the body he took pride in keeping so fit jammed skin to skin against hers. Inserting his hands between her thighs, he pressed them apart and then, opening his fly with a rough groan, he placed the tip of his heavily aroused sex at her most feminine core. Earlier…she'd *tasted* like heaven. Now he would find out if she *felt* like it too.

Arching up off of the floor, Maya let her slumberous, inviting glance fall hungrily into his. 'What are you waiting for?' she gasped. 'I want you so much… If you care about my sanity take me now…*please*…'

'Maya, you hardly have to ask… I'm all yours… *All* yours for however long you want me… I promise you.'

With one scalding hot thrust he filled her, and for the most dizzying unforgettable moment Blaise *did* lose his mind. She was exquisite…tight and silky as a hot satin glove. As he began to move deeper and harder inside her she whimpered, and again he kissed her, drowning out her erotic little cries with his demanding, voracious mouth, driving into her body as if it was the only destination he'd been seeking all his life and he would not soon relinquish it…

Maya had quickly come to terms with the realisation that all Blaise wanted was her body. *After all…why should he be different from any other man who had been interested in her?* Feeling upset by Blaise's remarks earlier, about adoring women but not finding one he wanted to commit to, Maya had stemmed the flood of emotion that threatened to unbalance her and given herself a firm reprimand. Facing the facts, she'd decided, was more empowering than succumbing yet again to grief and hurt because life had once more confirmed her worst fears—that she must indeed be unlovable. If this wild, tempestuous coupling was all she would ever have with Blaise then she would honestly accept it, and not wound herself further by wanting more.

In fact…tonight she'd decided she could be whoever she liked—for instance a passionate, daring woman who could truly be mature about what might turn out to be a hot one-night stand, or even several hot nights of passion, but who wouldn't rack herself with recriminations when the affair came to its inevitable end.

Now, as Blaise voraciously claimed her body, Maya's hands locked tight onto the impressive iron muscle in his shoulders—the touch of his skin warm and silky, his muscled forearms and lean torso dusted with a smattering of darkly golden hair through which she glimpsed his darker, flat male nipples. He was raining kisses on her mouth, her throat, her breasts, his seductive masculine scent and strong, hard body saturating her senses—making her forget that a world even existed outside this room. Wriggling beneath him on the carpet, Maya adjusted her slender body to accept his possession even deeper inside her, wrapping her long legs round his waist, one hand moving to the back of his neck to guide his lips voraciously back to hers whenever he removed them.

Somehow she'd become *addicted* to the taste of him. It seemed impossible that she would ever get enough of those scalding, inflammatory kisses... But suddenly Blaise tore his mouth from hers, to stare back into her eyes for a stunning moment that would be forever etched in her memory with the most exquisite clarity. Maya stared back, hardly knowing what to say or think. Then he delivered another one of those sexy, knowing little smiles of his, the azure blue eyes twinkling in the lamplight, making him look as if he'd invented the very word *temptation*...in fact was the *personification* of it. Then, slowly and deeply, he started to rock her hips towards his.

A stunned gasp was torn from her throat as her release came, quick and fast, stealing her breath as it convulsed her, even as Blaise's own movements started to match it. Her heart thumping hard enough to jump right out of her chest, Maya stared up at her lover, knowing the *exact* moment when his own powerful climax held him in thrall and sensing the scalding force of his seed spurt deep inside her.

They'd been so swept away by the power of the wild, raging river of need that engulfed them that neither of them had thought about protection.

Now, as she carefully lowered her legs to the floor again, her feet touching the soft carpet once more, she rested her hands on the smooth flesh of Blaise's back, sensing the slick rippling muscle beneath his skin contract and then still beneath her fingers. Her sigh of longing and resignation at what they'd done hovered softly on the air between them. She would never regret it, but would Blaise?

Scraping his fingers through his mane of gold hair, he ruefully moved his head from side to side, his gaze boring deeply down into hers. 'I'm so sorry, Maya... there's no excuse. I should have protected you, but you're so beautiful and incredible that the possibility of thinking straight around you went right out the window! I guess I just got rather carried away. If anything happens I—'

'Shh.' Maya put her fingers against his lips. 'I got carried away too, Blaise,' she confessed shyly, 'but don't worry...it's the wrong time of the month for anything to happen.'

'Next time I promise I'll take more care.' Smoothing her hair gently back from her forehead, Blaise was regarding her almost tenderly, making no sudden move to separate his body from hers despite his rueful confession that he should have used protection. In fact, to her great surprise, Maya already sensed him becoming aroused again inside her.

'Do you mean...like *now*?' she asked, wide-eyed.

'See what you do to me?'

His lips met hers in a long, lingering kiss that ignited the fireworks inside her all over again, but just as Maya started to surrender to more of the same drugging, irresistible lovemaking Blaise regretfully withdrew from her body.

'But I'm not doing this again without protecting you. I'm also concerned that you're going to get carpet burns if we stay on the floor like this! I think the bed might be more comfortable, don't you? You get in. Give me a couple of minutes and I'll be right back with what we need.' On his feet again, Blaise yanked up his trousers and did up his fly. Then he reached for Maya's hand to assist her. His wonderful chest was left provocatively bare.

Self-consciously, Maya drew the torn sides of her nightshirt together over her own naked breasts. 'Blaise?'

'What is it?' Immediately he moved in closer, sweeping the sides of her nightshirt aside and possessively cupping her hips with his warm, slightly callused hands as he concernedly examined her face.

'If you're coming back to bed…does that mean you'll be spending the night with me?'

His ensuing laugh was low and sensual, and almost rough with undisguised need. 'Try ejecting me, darling, and you'll have a genuine fight on your hands!'

'Good morning, my love!' The housekeeper paused in the kitchen doorway, clearly startled by the sight of Maya sitting with her chair pulled out from the pine table and the huge Irish Wolfhound lying at her feet, as though keeping guard over the lovely young brunette.

'You're up and about early. Give me a few minutes and I'll get you a nice cup of tea.'

'Don't bother about tea, Lottie, thanks all the same.' Getting to her feet, Maya dusted down her jeans. As if on cue, Sheba also rose, gazing up at her with an expression that looked like longing in her eyes. 'I thought I'd take Sheba for a bit of a walk before breakfast…is that all right?'

'Of course it's all right. My Tom usually takes her, but he'll be glad of a break this morning before he tackles the day's work, I'm sure. There's always plenty to do round a big place like this, and today he's mowing that huge front lawn. You don't need to bother with a lead, lass—just don't let madam here dictate the pace, or you'll come back fit for nothing!'

Out in the grounds, breathing in air that was akin to having pure oxygen injected into her lungs, Maya tramped grass still damp with morning dew. The Irish Wolfhound loped along beside her quite agreeably. Strangely, she found unexpected comfort and companionship in the animal's presence. She had never had a pet when she was a child— her father hadn't allowed it—but being around Sheba made her realise that she actually liked the idea. However, her thoughts did not dwell on the subject for long. Not when every cell in her body was still vibrating with the memory of Blaise's passionate loving last night, and her skin carried the tender spots to prove it.

Extricating herself from that warm, cosy bed this morning, she'd been so careful not to disturb him, but thankfully the calm, rhythmic rise and fall of his heavenly chest had indicated that he was enjoying the deepest of deep sleeps—one he wouldn't wake from in a hurry. The fact hardly surprised Maya when they'd spent most of the night lost in each other's arms, driven to greater and greater heights of ardent fervour by this— this *maelstrom* of need and desire that they seemed to generate so electrifyingly between them.

She'd risen early because she'd needed some time on her own to absorb what had occurred. Her only other lover had been Sean, and although she had lost her virginity to him he had hardly set her on fire with his quickly over with attentions. Even at the time Maya had known in her heart that her relationship with him had been nothing but a Band-Aid for what really ailed her…a deep, gnawing loneliness coupled with a sometimes desperate need for love that wouldn't go away.

But nothing could have prepared her for the passionate revelation that was Blaise Walker… Tugging open the neckline of her waterproof jackct, she sniffed. Even though she'd showered thoroughly, and washed her hair twice, it was as though he'd left his provocative masculine scent all over her… Or was she just imagining that was so because she'd simply not been able to get enough of him? Would a woman *ever* be able to get enough of such an incredible man? Now Maya knew that he'd ruined her for anyone else. Any other man she might be with in the future would only ever get barely a *quarter* of what she felt for Blaise. But even considering that there might be another man in her future was akin to feeling as if she was already betraying herself. She simply couldn't do it…not after what she'd just experienced. If this so-called affair of theirs *did* develop into something deeper on her part could she honestly handle it as easily as she seemed to be trying to convince herself that she could?

Sheba chose that moment to nudge her with that huge head of hers. It took Maya a couple of seconds to realise what she wanted. 'I'm sorry, poppet… I didn't think to bring a ball to throw for you.' She fondly ruffled the thick grey fur. 'Maybe I can find a stick for you instead? Come on, girl…let's go see what we can find, eh?'

Blaise drank his coffee, checked the time on his watch and gazed out of the window for the umpteenth time. He'd woken in a state of almost instant arousal at the thought of engaging Maya in some sexy, languorous early-morning lovemaking, and instead had been confused and disgruntled to find that she had already risen without him. As he'd swung his legs out of bed, then scraped his fingers through his hair, he'd quickly added frustration to the list of woes he was mentally compiling because of her desertion.

Walking into the kitchen, he had felt his jaw all but hit

the floor at Lottie's cheery announcement. 'Miss Hayward has taken Sheba for a walk…wasn't that kind of her?'

Kind? Blaise had echoed ironically. Abandoning him in preference to taking his dog for a walk wasn't kind…it was pure sadistic torment! Yet part of him knew an honest admiration for Maya too, at the realisation she was obviously trying to overcome a childhood fear by taking Sheba out.

He found himself reflecting on what a tough road she'd been travelling. Just the thought of that idiot that she'd gone out with who'd so clumsily revealed what he was up to, with an accidental text to Maya's mobile phone, made Blaise want to find him and teach him a lesson he wouldn't soon forget!

Then, realising that the idea had been generated by a too-easy familiar fury sweeping through him, he experienced genuine revulsion that he was perhaps becoming more like his father every day. Clenching his jaw, he shook his head, as if to rid himself of such a demoralising, painful thought. Now, hearing Maya's velvet-soft voice in the hallway in brief conversation with Tom, another far more agreeable sensation gripped him instead. With almost bated breath he waited for her to come through the kitchen doorway.

'Hi there.' Her smile was a little lopsided—almost *shy*—but to Blaise's eyes she looked simply wonderful, with her pink cheeks, her dark hair mussed by the wind, dressed in well-worn jeans and a red waterproof jacket.

'Good morning.' He sauntered across to her, not hesitating to tug her gently but firmly into his arms. 'You deserted me. I woke up and there you were... gone.'

'I just—I just needed some fresh air, so I took Sheba with me for a walk. The grounds here are really beautiful—just like a stately home.'

'With the aid of a couple of part-time gardeners Tom does a sterling job taking care of it all. But let's not talk about the grounds or the gardens, hmm?'

'I think we should talk about the play. I can't wait to get started on the research today.'

To Blaise's chagrin, Maya ducked out of the way of his intended kiss, and stepped out of his embrace too.

'So it's to be all business, is it?' He knew he sounded unreasonably annoyed—almost *petulant*—but right then he didn't care. 'Just as if last night never happened?'

Maya frowned. 'I want to do a good job for you, Blaise—remember I told you that? And I don't want you to think that I'm somehow expecting special privileges because we slept together either. I'm here to work, and that's how I intend to proceed from now on.'

'Really?' Irritation made Blaise feel like breaking something. He could hardly believe she was acting so cool with him...as if she'd just had a one-night stand she was quickly regretting, instead of being consumed by the thought of how soon they could get together again, as *he* was.

Maya didn't answer him...just stood there calmly unzipping her jacket.

'Well, if that's the way you want it, then so be it. Get yourself some breakfast, then come and find me in my study. I'll expect to see you there in exactly twenty minutes...no later!'

As he headed out of the room, he was so mad that he could hardly bring himself to look at her...

CHAPTER NINE

WHEN Maya turned up in Blaise's study, just under twenty minutes later, it was to find him writing furiously away in long-hand at his desk. She knew he must have heard her enter, but he didn't glance up to acknowledge her presence for at least two or three minutes. Already aware he was not very happy with her, but also aware that an artist at work should never be disturbed unless it was an emergency—a rule that had been drummed into her by her father—she deliberately kept quiet.

To be honest, it was no hardship for Maya just to watch him. Although she kept experiencing an almost irresistible urge to touch him…to slide her hand round that exquisite sculpted jaw and bring his mouth close to hers, so that she could tease and taste and remind herself of what she'd so freely enjoyed doing last night. But because he looked so serious she also wanted to brush back that rogue lock of dark gold hair from his forehead as he bent over his large spiral notebook and make him look at her instead.

Eventually, he did glance up. There followed an uncomfortable moment when Maya felt like a blundering insensitive stranger who had walked in on him.

'You took your time,' he commented grumpily. 'Pull out that chair and sit down. Got something to write in?'

'No—yes… I mean give me a second.' She dashed into the adjoining office to sweep a notebook and pen off the top of the desk. A little red-faced, she returned and drew out a chair, her notepad and pen at the ready.

'Before we start,' he began, his intense, all but scorching blue gaze closely examining her, 'do up the top buttons on your shirt.'

'What?' Embarrassed, in case her blouse had unwittingly come undone and she was revealing more flesh than was seemly, Maya saw that the buttons were fastened almost right up to her neck. Only the very top one was left free, and all that revealed was the slender column of her throat.

'There's just one button not secured, and I'm not fastening that because it makes me feel too claustrophobic'

'Well, then, go and put something on that's a little less provocative.'

'What? It's a perfectly respectable blouse and not the least bit provocative!' Defensively, Maya touched her hand to her chest. Instantly she saw that Blaise's gaze go straight there and his jaw tightened.

'Well, *I* find it provocative!'

'That's hardly my fault.'

'It is your fault,' he insisted belligerently, 'because you chose to wear the damn thing!'

'This is ridiculous. You're only behaving like this because—'

'Because what, Maya? I'd really like to hear your thoughts on the matter.'

She squirmed uncomfortably as a wave of scorching heat all but glued her to the chair. 'It's because—oh, I don't know!'

'Liar.'

'All right, then. You find what I'm wearing provocative because clearly you're frustrated,' she exclaimed in exasperation, wishing that just looking at him didn't drive every other thought from her head other than the one that said she wanted him so badly it hurt.

'Damn right I'm frustrated,' he replied, and there was a lascivious gleam in his eye that made Maya squirm even more. 'How in hell am I supposed to work when just the sight of you is driving me crazy?'

Not knowing how to answer that question, Maya examined her linked hands in her lap and felt everything—including the tips of her ears—burn.

'Perhaps…'

Getting up, Blaise walked slowly round the desk to join her—reached out and started gently massaging her shoulder. Feeling her body *and* her resolve melt at his touch, Maya was momentarily dazzled by the glint of a gold signet ring set with a diamond that he wore on his little finger.

'Perhaps what?' she asked, turning to regard him.

'Perhaps between the two of us we can find a way to alleviate some of my frustration…before we start work, I mean…' His voice was huskily sinful. It rolled over her like tropical waves of heat lapping at the shore of her already highly sensitised body.

'Blaise, please don't—'

'Please don't what?'

He was smoothing his hands down the sides of her arms, his palms glancing deliberately against her breasts. Hot needles of pleasure and desire caused Maya's nipples to surge and prickle to the point of pain inside her bra.

'This is madness, Blaise. I can't—I can't think straight when you do things like that to me.'

'I'm not asking you to think.'

'But I'm here to work, not to—not to succumb to your highly provocative ways of distracting me!'

'No?'

He bent to kiss her, but Maya stoically turned her face away at the last moment, and his intended kiss glanced off the side of her mouth instead.

'We—you really need to work, and I'm meant to be helping you.'

There was a well-timed—or perhaps *not* so well-timed—knock at the door. Stepping instantly away from her side, Blaise cursed softly under his breath.

'Come in!' he called out, his tone definitely disgruntled.

Lottie walked in, carrying a tray with a full cafetière alongside a plate of biscuits. 'Thought you might like some coffee to keep you both going while you work,' she said brightly, carefully depositing the tray on the desk.

'Thanks, that's great.'

Her employer's smile was tense. Maya knew he was definitely put out by the intrusion. The housekeeper glanced sideways at her. 'That's a very pretty blouse you're wearing, my dear.'

'Thank you.' Maya didn't dare look at Blaise after this comment. However, Lottie's interruption did give her some valuable time to restore common sense to the situation, and she seized the opportunity to effect some much needed distance between them, even knowing he would probably taunt her about it later.

'Excuse me, but I need to go and sort out which books I'll need for our research.'

'For God's sake, Maya, I—'

But she'd already left the room before Blaise had even finished the sentence.

Maya had absolutely done the right thing, disappearing for a while. Blaise had had no choice but to get down to some work. It wasn't easy when his mind was taunted by too erotic images of her, but once he started to write the story totally absorbed him, drawing him into the drama that was unfolding on the cinema screen of his mind and making him forget everything—even *her*.

Yet that wasn't completely true. In the play, the female lead of the piece had helplessly turned into Maya, and Blaise found to his surprise that he was becoming more and more emotionally involved in the character than with any other female part he had ever written. *It was a strange process, what he did for a living.* He believed he was far more capable of expressing emotion in his writing than he was in day-to-day life. Subconsciously he supposed he blamed his parents for that. God knew they'd expressed enough stormy emotion throughout their married life to make any child of theirs either abhor it or shun replicating it as far as possible.

Disturbingly uncomfortable echoes from the past gripped him for a few frozen moments...so much so that he swore he could hear his mother's anguished cries coming back down the years to haunt him. Such an incident had not occurred for ages. He couldn't help wondering why memories of his not so happy family should surface now. Determinedly, Blaise refocused on his work. After writing a particularly stirring scene between his female lead and her soldier suitor, he reached for the half-full cafetière and poured himself another cup of coffee. At least two hours had passed since Lottie had made it, and the dark bitter brew was barely warm, but he drank it all the same, mulling deeply over the words he had put onto the page in front of him.

The door to the connecting office opened and Maya reappeared.

'I don't want to disturb you, but I've been looking through some of the books on my shelf and making notes about what you might need—it's just an educated guess, I'm afraid, since we haven't discussed it in any length, but I thought I'd go upstairs to the library and see what I could find there.'

'Maya?'

'Yes?'

Blaise found himself hypnotised by her wide innocent gaze. 'I've scribbled down a short list of some things that might be useful.' Tearing out a page from his own book, he held it out to her. Glancing down at the contents, she couldn't hide the unfeigned excitement in her eyes, causing him to muse silently that she was the first woman he'd been intimately involved with who had expressed a genuine interest in his work. A frisson of unashamed pride and pleasure rippled through him.

'I'll crack on, then.'

'Take your time. We'll catch up later and talk over what you've got. I'll also need you to type out what I've done today.'

'That won't be a hardship. I'd love to see how the story's progressing.' Reaching the door that led into the hallway, Maya paused to venture a friendly smile. 'I hope the writing is going well for you,' she said encouragingly.

'I'm not doing badly so far.' He grinned back. 'By

the way, I didn't congratulate you on conquering your fear around dogs and taking Sheba for a walk earlier.'

'I loved being with her. And I think it's just like you said it would be…somehow I got the sense that she's looking after me and wants to protect me.'

Did she but know it, the expression on her face just then was like a lost little girl who'd just been found, and all Blaise's suppressed longing for her of that morning came hurtling back to the fore again…

When Maya arrived upstairs, a cloak of silence descended like muffled snow all around her. As she walked down the long, stately corridor towards the library, a shiver chased down her spine. *There were ghosts here…just like she'd sensed when they'd been walking by the wall outside…* Only these weren't ghosts of marching Roman soldiers—these were ghosts of family now gone.

She wondered why Blaise barely talked about his parents. After all, he had inherited the family home, and had already told her he'd lived here with them when he was young. Had something unpleasant happened between them? He'd already indicated that his father had had an explosive temper. Was that why he seemed so reticent about discussing his childhood?

Frowning, Maya reached the library and pushed open the door. It was cool inside and, tucking her pad against her chest, she folded her arms to get warm. The room was stunning, decorated in the style of its

Jacobean ancestry, but with some smart contemporary pieces of furniture dotted around too. Best of all, it was lined with bookshelves from floor to ceiling that were jam-packed with books, and in the middle of the far wall was the most beautiful inlaid marble fireplace. Above it hung a striking portrait of a handsome young dark-haired man. Moving closer to examine the picture, Maya felt a jolt a bit like a small lightning strike, jagged through her insides. The name of the artist was scrawled at the bottom right-hand corner, plain for all to see…*Alistair Devereaux.*

How did Blaise come to own one of her father's paintings? Why had he never told her about it? Studying the painting, with its exquisite confident brushstrokes and bold use of colour, Maya was catapulted back in time. Suddenly memories of all her father had meant to her—his love for her, his neglect of her and finally his complete and utter desertion of her—crashed down over her head. Furiously wiping her tears away, she was poignantly struck right then by how dangerously strong her feelings were becoming towards Blaise.

She should look out. If she got too close to him would *he* ultimately neglect her, reject her and desert her? Why shouldn't he do all those things? she asked herself. He was in the arts, as her father had once been, was well known by the media and fêted by an adoring public. What she knew of him so far seemed to suggest that he was fairly wary of commitment too… She'd be an utter idiot to let her heart be ensnared by such a man—no matter how charming, handsome, talented or good in bed. She'd best just stick to her resolve of having an affair and expect nothing else…*because she knew without a doubt that her self-preservation depended on it*…

At dinner that night, after what had turned out to be a very satisfying day's work, Blaise returned his half-drunk glass of Chardonnay to the table, avidly studying Maya's softly shadowed features in the flickering candlelight.

'By the way, tomorrow I'm giving you a car for your use while you're here. I thought you might like another MG, since you seem to know so much about them. What do you think?' he asked.

Carefully Maya touched her white linen napkin to her lips. She was wearing a very becoming multi-coloured maxi-dress, its swirls of soft verdant green in the pattern of the satiny material complementing the vivid emerald of her eyes, and Blaise found himself admiringly musing if there was a colour in existence that didn't complement her? He very much doubted it.

'Are you sure? If it's anything like the one we drove to Camden in it must be your pride and joy.'

'I trust that you're not going to be reckless and drive it into a brick wall. And if you do…' He lifted his broad shoulders in a careless shrug. 'I think I'll get over it. At the end of the day it's only a car.'

'My father was extremely possessive and protective

about his cars. If any one of them had been damaged in any way, I don't think he would have got over it so easily.'

'Was he as possessive and protective about you?'

'I think you already know the answer to that question.' She gazed at him steadily, and there was an air of defiance about her unwavering stare. When Blaise didn't probe further, she sighed, saying, 'I have a question for *you*. Why didn't you tell me you owned one of my father's paintings? The one in the library—though for all I know you may have others you haven't told me about.'

'I only have the one. The portrait of a young actor my father was mentoring. It was left to me when my parents died. To tell you the truth, I did plan on telling you about it, but I guess I just got wrapped up in work and forgot.'

'You didn't think I'd be interested in such a pertinent piece of information, seeing as the painter *was* my father?'

'Seems to me you have a lot of unresolved business concerning your father, Maya, and I get the feeling it really haunts you.'

'And it seems to me that you have a lot of unresolved business concerning your past too, Blaise! Or else why are you so reluctant to even talk about it? It's like you've built some kind of—of fortress around the subject, with a sign saying "Keep out".'

Inside his chest, Blaise's heartbeat accelerated. He'd been anticipating some pleasant and relaxed small talk over dinner, before finally doing the thing he craved the most…taking Maya to bed and enjoying a long, unin-terrupted breathless night's lovemaking. What he *hadn't* been anticipating was that she would be challenging him on the one part of his life that he kept strictly private. The one topic that *wasn't* open to casual after-dinner conversation. He twisted his lips into a grimace.

'We all have skeletons in the closet, Maya. Why don't we just leave mine where they are?'

'What are you so afraid of? Aren't playwrights supposed to be bold and daring? Aren't they interested in exploring the mistakes of the past? Isn't that what you're doing in the play you're writing now?'

'What about your father's mistakes?' Blaise demanded, sensing his temper rise. 'It's clear you've been pretty damaged by them. What the hell good does it do to keep on revisiting the past? Answer me that!'

Across the table, Maya's shoulders drooped a little in an expression of defeat. 'You're right. I probably *am* damaged by what my father did—the way he lived and the way he died. I suppose I'm just trying to understand it all, really…that's all. I'm trying to understand it so that if I have children of my own I won't ever do what he did—put myself and my career and my so-called friends first, so much so that the children are neglected and left to fend for themselves. I'll show them every day that they mean the world to me, and love them so much that they'll never have a moment's doubt that they're not my top priority—no matter what else is going on in my life!'

Seeing the determination *and* distress mirrored in her lovely features, Blaise felt his heart helplessly contract. Recalling his own father's vile temper, and what the consequences of that had been like for him and his mother, he realised his home life had been a *fairytale* compared to what Maya had been through. There were no doubts in his mind that she would make a terrific mother one day…not to mention a wonderful wife to some very, very fortunate man.

'I found his body after he'd hung himself,' she told him softly.

CHAPTER TEN

SHAKING his head in disbelief, Blaise sensed his stomach violently turn over. 'What?'

Maya stared down at the table. Her long dark hair fell gently forward, partially shielding her.

'He was in his studio… I'd just returned from buying some groceries—he never thought about food when he was working and the cupboard was bare.' She glanced up and grimaced. 'I called out to him but he didn't answer. I knew he was working, trying his best to get something new going after a long period of not being able to work at all, so I put the food away and made us both a cup of tea.'

'You don't have to go on if this is too painful.'

'I want to. I haven't spoken to anyone about it for a long time, and I—and I need to.'

'Then I want to listen.'

'Anyway…I knocked on the door and called out again—not so loud as to disturb him from his train of thought, just clear enough that he could hear me. Still he didn't answer. I carefully opened the door and glanced in.'

Her chin wobbled a little, and Blaise's breath was suddenly trapped inside his chest.

'He was hanging by a rope he'd tied onto the chandelier—it was a fairly hefty, lavish affair—and little shards of glass lay shattered and broken beneath his feet on the table that he'd dragged over so that he could—so that he could—' Covering her face with her hand, she began to cry softly.

For a frozen second Blaise couldn't make himself move. Then he was on his feet, moving swiftly round to her side, pulling her gently upright and guiding her head down onto his chest. Almost immediately her hot tears dampened his shirt, and he rained tender little kisses over her silken hair, breathing in her sweetly perfumed shampoo and feeling her slender body shudder against him.

'Cry as much as you want to, sweetheart,' he crooned. 'I won't let you go. I'll just keep on holding you.'

'This isn't what you hired me for…to behave like some emotional wreck and have you take care of me.'

'Are you crazy? Do you honestly think it's a hardship for me to hold you like this after what we've shared?'

'All these years,' she whispered against his shirt, 'I've kept on thinking that if I'd only got back sooner… or if I hadn't gone to the shops at all…he might—he might still be here…'

'No, Maya…sweetheart, I think you're wrong.'

'How do you know?' Trustingly, hopefully, she raised her face to his.

Folding his palms round her slim upper arms, Blaise breathed in deeply. 'It sounds like he'd let himself descend too low into the pit of despair to be rescued by anyone…' Unable to resist, he traced the tracks of her tears with the pad of his thumb. 'Least of all you. He was meant to take care of you, Maya…not the other way round.'

'What if he tried his best to take care of me but he just couldn't? I can't keep on blaming him for that.'

Even now she was still protecting him, Blaise realised with incredulity. After all the man had put her through!

'You don't have to keep on blaming him, but he absolutely did not try his best to take care of you, Maya. Whatever you say, however much you may want to jump to his defence, he didn't try his best at all. He may have been an incredible artist, but it was his only daughter he should have lavished his love and devotion on first…even before his art.'

'To be honest, I think that sometimes he used his painting to escape the world—but don't we all do that in one form or another at times of stress or worry? Try to escape? Can I tell you something else? I don't always feel so forgiving towards him. Sometimes I *hate* him for what he did…how he behaved, how he put people who didn't even care about him before me. But the truth is I also loved him very much.'

'Most relationships are that complicated.'

'You know the strangest thing? After his funeral I had the strongest sense that he was looking after me at last. Instead of going to pieces, which is how I feared I might react, I felt this really warm sensation of peace and love wrap itself round me. It stayed with me for months…even when everything had to be sold to pay off his debts and I was forced to leave our home.'

'Where did you go?'

'A friend of mine was sharing a house with two other girls and they offered me a room. A couple of months before that—knowing that my father was in financial difficulty—I'd left school and got myself a job in an office, so that I could help support us. Anyway…'

She shrugged matter-of-factly, and her lips formed a tentative smile. As subtle as the gesture was, the sweet curve of her lips acted like a ray of pure sunlight, dazzling him.

'You're perfectly right. It doesn't do any good to keep revisiting the past—it can be an exercise doomed to make you miserable. It's what's happening now that we need to concentrate on, isn't it? I've told myself not to keep dwelling on things, and I *do* want to try and put everything that happened behind me, but still…it was a terrible thing, you know? To witness, I mean…'

'To even *imagine* it is terrible enough, Maya. And you had to cope with that devastating event all on your own. That takes tremendous courage.'

'I suppose I've never thought about it like that before. That I had courage... But I must have had it even to want to continue. And I have continued...I haven't given up. *I'm* still here and I have to count my blessings. I've got the rest of my life to live, right? I'm determined to put my whole self into whatever I do next—not have only half of me show up, which I think is what I've been doing all these years. It's time to move away from all the sadness—to go forward with a bit more optimism.'

'If anyone can do that, *you* can, Maya.'

'Blaise?'

'Hmm?'

'Thank you.'

'For what?'

'Listening.'

Her gratitude almost undid him—particularly when he thought it was singularly undeserved. 'Any time.'

'If *you* ever need someone to just listen...I'll be there for you too.'

Steadily he rested his gaze on her lovely face, but said nothing.

'I don't know why, but sometimes I get the feeling there's something from the past that really bothers you, Blaise. You don't show it outwardly—I mean you're very confident and successful at what you do—but it's just a sense I get. Is it—is it to do with your family?'

Stultifying mental shadows pressed close, and his

usual battle with the tide of hurtful memory gripped Blaise in a vice. 'Another time,' he replied gruffly. 'Another time perhaps I'll talk to you about it.'

Lowering his glance, he saw the doubt in her eyes and knew she had every right to doubt him. Resistance to discussing both his family and his fears about repeating his father's reprehensible behaviour was so strong in him that he took the path of avoidance every time...*every time*. Inside, he bitterly despaired that he would ever be any different.

The truth was that Maya was far more courageous than he could ever hope to be. She was willing to deal with the dark cloud of memory that sometimes enveloped her, had made a pact to try and move away from it, to be more optimistic about life. Perhaps all Blaise could do was keep on pouring his stifled emotion into his work instead? And maybe he should properly confront the fact that in all likelihood he would spend the rest of his life alone because of his inability to face up to things. One thing he was certain of: he would not venture into a long-term commitment with a woman with such a high risk of failure hanging over his head. *For who would stay with a man that might potentially harm them?* He especially wouldn't do that to a woman like Maya—someone who had already been hurt almost beyond imagining.

Maybe he had been selfish to embark on this passionate odyssey with her? She surely deserved better than just enjoying some explosive sex with a man who—despite his genuine concern for her—fully intended to kiss her goodbye some time soon? When she'd talked about her ex he had heard disappointment and hurt in her voice that her imagined happy future with him had come to naught, and in such a cruelly painful way too. Surely a short affair with Blaise would only confirm her opinion that all men were louses? *Users…who didn't give a damn about her as long as they got what they wanted?*

Dropping his hands to rest them lightly either side of her hips in her long satin dress, Blaise couldn't resist impelling her body closer to his, even though he was in turmoil about his right to intimacy with Maya at all.

Her scent made him feel hypnotised…drugged. And he wanted her again, with no lessening of the fierce need and burning desire that had seized him from almost the first moment he saw her. Reverently he touched his lips to her infinitely soft cheek.

'Let me take you to bed, Maya. It won't make the hurt go away, but it might help you forget for a while… And the truth is I need to make love to you… need it more than anything else in the world right now…'

When he reached out his hand for hers, Maya hesitated only a moment before silently slipping her palm into his…

Her fingers splayed lightly across Blaise's hipbone, Maya snuggled closer to his wonderful naked masculine form in the bed. 'Your skin feels like rough warm silk,' she told him, smiling up into his handsome face in the lamplight.

'And yours…there are no words to do such delicious softness justice. Except perhaps to say that I think heaven must feel like this. You're a revelation to me, you know? Yes, a revelation—as well as one very irresistible and tempting woman, Maya Hayward.'

'How tempting?' She touched him in the place where he was most sensitive and *most* aroused. Beneath her gently exploring fingers she sensed the warm silken length of his manhood pulse even harder into life. They had already shared some of the most combustible languorous kisses Maya could imagine—her lips still bore the exquisite aftermath of his alternately demanding then gentle mouth. Now she watched him rip open a slim foil packet to release the protective sheath inside, his brief examination of her teasing expression hot, libidinous and hungry.

'Climb on top and I'll show you, sweetheart.'

'You mean sometimes actions speak louder than words…even for a playwright?' She grinned.

Along with her seemingly insatiable desire for this man, there was a new lightness and playfulness skipping through her bloodstream that she hadn't known was even possible. Loving the sensation of her inner thighs gripping Blaise's lean, arrow-straight hips, she didn't take her gaze off his as he thrust upwards inside her with devastating intent. His blue eyes were like living, dangerous electricity, and she immediately felt him fill her to the hilt. He stayed there, rocking her gently, so that she was intimately acquainted with every wonderful inch of him, his hands clasping her hips.

Her head momentarily falling back, Maya shut her eyes. That sense of lightness pulsing through her body wasn't just because she'd finally decided to leave the past behind and move on…*it was because she was in love, she realised.* Her eyes shot open again. Blaise might not yet trust her enough to share whatever it was that troubled him, and he might have clearly hinted that he wasn't a man who welcomed long-term commitment either, but there it was. *She loved him.* Hugging the knowledge to her, she gazed down at him with a new sense of wonder and appreciation.

'Hey,' he said, his seductively low-pitched voice breaking a little, 'keep on looking at me like that and you may just have to stay right where you are for the rest of the night. Think you could handle that?'

Leaning towards Maya, he cupped her face, drawing her mouth urgently down to his before she could reply. As the heat and hardness of his demanding kiss avidly claimed her, she willingly returned his passionate fervour with all her heart, suddenly finding herself praying hard that one day, despite her intention to only enjoy a brief affair, he might love her back…that his love might lead to the dream of a happy, fulfilling union with a man that constantly eluded her.

'I think I could handle anything you wanted to give me, Mr Walker,' she murmured, nuzzling her face deep into the beguiling warmth of his neck…

He was outside walking by the wall again, with the wind in his hair and—it had to be said—a spring in his step. He didn't waste time speculating *why*. The reason was back at the house, eagerly continuing research for the play on Blaise's behalf and by all accounts loving every minute of it. It had taken a monumental effort on his part not to say to hell with it and keep Maya in bed for the rest of the day. But the plain fact of the matter was that he had a play to write, and it wouldn't progress any further if he lost himself in any more distractions…*delightful and engaging as they might be*.

No, he needed to delve deeper into his protagonist's character, needed to see what else it was besides a dream of a more exciting future that drove him to leave his family and join up with the Roman army, to travel to a foreign land and guard a border he had never even seen before.

After an hour and a bit of walking across the uneven crags, he felt the wind pick up and become ever more gusting as he passed the odd intrepid fellow walker on the way. Then finally, his head down and his mind intent on developing the storyline, Blaise had his answer. When it came he sucked in a breath and sensed his insides roll over.

It had been there all the time, hovering on the edge of his consciousness from the moment he'd come up with the play's concept, but unbelievably he had been playing the avoidance game again. Now it seemed there was no longer any place left to hide...

'How's the play going?'

'Hello, Jane.' Blaise rocked back in his chair with the phone receiver next to his ear and grinned. 'How's life in the great metropolis?'

'Answer my question first, and then I'll tell you.'

'The play's going fine. For the past two weeks I've hit a real blue streak.'

'Inspired, no doubt, by your visiting muse? How is she, by the way? The fact that she's still with you after two weeks and hasn't high-tailed it back to London tells me a lot.'

'Does it, indeed?'

'Yes—it tells me about her tenacity, for one thing...as well as about her resilience in continuing to work in the face of how temperamental and demanding you artistic types can be.'

Blaise frowned. 'Her father was an artist,' he said thoughtfully.

'That explains it, then. You're utterly charming and beguiling, darling, but we both know that when you're working sparks of artistic temperament are apt to fly!'

'I've changed!' he said jokingly. Then a second later

realised he meant it. He *had* changed since he'd been around Maya. She'd definitely been responsible for bringing out a much more mellow side in him—a side where he was a little less angry when things didn't immediately go his way, where he could actually relax in a woman's company and not feel the need to escape and be on his own at some point.

'She's great, by the way,' he remarked, finally answering Jane's question. Even just thinking about Maya made him grow warm. Right now she was in the adjoining office, typing up yesterday's work, and later that afternoon he was taking her into town so that they could enjoy tea at a five-star hotel.

'My, my…' Jane's voice lowered meaningfully. 'How the mighty are fallen.'

'What do you mean?'

'Are you falling for this girl, Blaise? I mean… *really* falling?'

He rocked forward again, feeling the skin between his brows pucker. 'You know I don't do happy-ever-after, Jane, so don't go getting your hopes up and looking at hats to wear to my wedding, will you?'

'You sound happier than usual—that's all I meant. When you talk about this woman your voice lights up.'

'Happiness doesn't last…*especially* where romantic relationships are concerned. Living with someone day after day is apt to take the rose-tinted edge off the illusion…or so I've heard. Why can't I simply enjoy what I have right now with Maya without it necessarily having to lead somewhere?'

'That's your prerogative, of course. Speaking as a friend, I just don't want to see you grow old and lonely on your own, I guess.'

'Well, I appreciate your concern, but do you honestly believe there *won't* be pretty and obliging women around to keep me company—*even* into my dotage?' Blaise chuckled, but the sound had a definitely *hollow* ring to it, even to his own ears...

CHAPTER ELEVEN

Maya stared at the pretty watercolour of violets on the wall by the door to Blaise's office, feeling stunned and faint. She wished she could erase from her mind the words she'd just heard Blaise speak but knew that it was impossible. It was obvious now that she'd merely been deluding herself that he was beginning to feel something deeper for her because they'd been spending more and more time together. The bond she'd imagined they shared was nothing but a foolish and ridiculous pipedream on her part!

All their liaison had probably been about for a dedicated commitment-phobe like Blaise was great sex.

Shockwaves of distress and pain rolled sickeningly through her. With her hands shaking, she put down the sheaf of paper she had just printed out to add to the small growing pile on the desk that was the play, then opened the door to step out into the adjoining office.

Having finished his phone conversation, Blaise

glanced up and saw her. He was dressed in his trade-mark black again, the sombre colour somehow render-ing him impossibly charismatic, adding a hint of seductive danger to good-looks that were already off-the-scale compelling. It also highlighted the dazzling glints of gold in his hair and the intense Mediterranean blue of his eyes. *The quick, easy smile on his handsome face all but broke Maya's heart.*

'I'm—I'm up to date with the typing and printing out,' she told him, desperately trying to control the quaver in her voice. 'I'd like to get a breath of fresh air now, if you don't mind?'

Eyes narrowing, Blaise got up and walked round the desk to join her. 'Is everything all right?'

'Of course.'

'Maya?' he pressed, clearly not believing her.

Twisting her hands in front of her, she suddenly couldn't contain the pain that was tearing her up inside and sensed it helplessly spill over.

'I was just wondering if I'd outstayed my welcome… if it wasn't time for some other "pretty and obliging" woman to replace me?'

The colour drained from his face. 'I was talking to my agent…you were listening to that?'

'Not intentionally.' She lifted her chin. 'I was about to come and tell you that I needed to get out for a while and inadvertently I heard you talking. It wasn't easy to hear…what you said, I mean…but I'm glad I heard you say it all the same. It was the wake-up call I needed. I'd rather dangerously started to fool myself about us, you see.'

'What about *us*?'

Did she imagine it, or was there suddenly a steely undertone to his voice? A firming of the fortress he had already built around his heart to keep out would-be threats to his emotions? Her spirits sank even lower.

'We're more than just two people working to-gether—we've become lovers. I know I said I only wanted an affair, but naively I started to think that after enjoying intimacy together night after night it might make you want something a bit more. I thought that things had been progressing a little deeper between us than my just being your temporary assistant and bedmate.'

'You *do* mean more to me than that, Maya…much more. You're an exceptional and beautiful woman, and I find myself in awe of what you've had to overcome in life to even get this far. I couldn't have accomplished what I've done so far on the play without you, and—'

'Let me finish.' She folded her arms across her chest, and her hurt glance was withering. 'And my contribution has been invaluable? Was that what you were going to say next? For God's sake, you make me sound like some naïve little schoolgirl who should be grateful for every crumb of praise and attention you deign to throw my way!'

'As wonderful as it's been, I thought you knew—

thought you realised that even though we're sleeping together this isn't going to be a permanent situation.'

Blaise's words fell on the air like daggers, slicing Maya in two. Lifting the heavy weight of her dark hair off the back of her neck, she pursed her lips, fielding the waves of pain that made her whole body tremble with distress.

'Sometimes a situation can change from—from what you expected into something else…something even *better*…if you let it…' she offered quietly.

When Blaise's intense examination of her turned into the deepest frown, making her sense both his regret *and* frustration that she was instigating a situation he was clearly uncomfortable with and probably deplored, a shattering moment of shocking self-discovery assailed her. *She was no different from her father…for she too had become an addict.* Yes, she'd become addicted to a man who clearly only wanted her for the pleasure her body could give him—and even that for just a brief time. For, after she'd gone, Maya was certain it wouldn't be long before Blaise found himself another 'adoring and willing' woman to warm his bed.

Because she had this terrible aching need to experience real love from a man she'd allowed herself to be seduced by him—even when in her heart she'd always known their liaison was doomed not to last. And when he had shown such depth of understanding and compassion towards her after hearing about her difficult and painful past, she'd fooled herself into believing that he must really care for her. That was why his announcement that he'd thought she *knew* their relationship was not destined to last had struck her like a hammer-blow. What a blind fool she'd been! How could she once more have made the same destroying mistake in a relationship? Would she ever be able to trust her instincts again? Swallowing hard, Maya knew all she could do right then was think about leaving and chalk up her experience as another painful dalliance with the universally recognised school of hard knocks.

'Maya, listen…' Blaise was saying. 'You deserve the best man that's out there. Someone who can be the real hero I sense you need. But that man isn't me.' Regretfully he shook his head, dropping his hands in a futile gesture to his arrow-straight hips. 'I don't want you to go, and I'm not looking to replace you with anyone else—I swear it. But neither do I want to lead you on and make you hope for something that I'm just not in a position to deliver.'

'Because you refuse to let a woman get close enough to even try? What you're telling me is that you'd rather just "adore" as many women as possible and let the chance or possibility of something more enduring…something more *meaningful*…pass you by? That sounds like a pretty lonely, not to mention *empty* existence to me, if you don't mind my saying so. Not that you give a damn *what* I think! And by the way…you've got me all wrong.'

With her heart pounding loud enough in her chest for

her to hear every unhappy beat, Maya squared up to Blaise without flinching.

'I'm not looking for a hero. All I want is a man who's willing to spend the rest of his life with me because he loves me. I'm not looking for perfection. Just someone a little flawed, like myself, who'll be as accepting of my less than perfect qualities as I would be of his. We'd work together to try and overcome them. And finally I want someone who doesn't believe the grass is greener some-where else—who is happy with what he already has. I want a man with the innate capacity to be loyal, as *I* would be loyal to him. I'm going out for that walk in the fresh air now, and when I get back I'll be packing my bags.'

She turned at the door, jerking her head towards the office she'd been occupying. 'By the way, you'll find the work I did this morning on my desk. You'll have to hire somebody else to type out the rest, but I'm sure as long as she does what you want, is easy on the eye and obliging, you'll hardly even notice that it's not me!'

New York, six weeks later

'Want to go for a beer or a cocktail somewhere?' Shrug-ging into his cashmere coat in the theatre foyer, amid the crush of well-wishers and the congratulatory smiles of satisfied patrons, critics and colleagues, Blaise felt distinctly uneasy as his diminutive agent gave him one of her slow 'I've got you taped' assessing glances.

'That lonely apartment you've been living in for the past month getting to you already?' she probed, her small, cropped blonde head erect, hazel eyes narrowed like a cat about to pounce on some poor unsuspecting mouse.

'I can get as much company as I need whenever I choose,' he snapped back, glancing round as a pretty redhead squeezed deliberately by him—one of the ensemble actresses in the production—giving him both a coy and invitational smile before reluctantly disappearing through the rotating theatre doors when he didn't respond.

'That's hardly in dispute, darling,' Jane replied, eyes rolling. The edges of her scarlet painted mouth softened somewhat. 'But when your mind is fixed on one particular person's company alone not even Angelina Jolie herself could fill the gap. Heard from her at all since you came to New York…? Your sad-eyed raven-haired little temporary assistant, I mean?'

'No.' Appalled at how bleak he sounded, Blaise shifted from one lean hip to the other. 'She has no idea that I left the UK a month ago. But then why should she? After she left I didn't keep in contact. It was only after spending two impossible weeks in Northumberland trying to work on that damn play alone that I decided I finally couldn't stand it and came here.'

Reaching for his usual acerbic humour to deflect any further near-the-knuckle questions from Jane, he defensively squared his jaw.

'Are you thirsty or aren't you? Even the most faded

blooms appreciate the odd drink of water to stop them from shrivelling up and dying, so I'm told!'

She whacked him with her shiny patent leather designer handbag—*hard*.

The foyer had emptied quickly, and outside on the sidewalk umbrellas were hurriedly opening to face the downpour that was spilling from the skies onto the somewhat chilly New York night.

'Faded bloom, my backside! At least I'm going back to my hotel to the man I've been married to for twenty years and who still thinks I hung the moon! Whereas *you*...'

Rubbing his arm where she'd hit him, Blaise scowled. 'Whereas *I* am apparently destined to walk into the sunset alone...*boo-hoo*. No doubt you think I deserve it.' He shook his head as if to shake off the deepening sense of gloom that made him feel heavy as concrete.

For six long weeks he hadn't even had the guts to pick up the phone and speak to Maya, let alone beg her for-giveness...which was exactly what he should have done. Instead he'd let her leave, as if she was as dispensable and replaceable as one of the stack of inexpensive pens he kept in his desk drawer. He either had to face the fact that he was too scared to overcome the childhood fears his family life had left him with, give them up and move on—or realise that he was a genuine twenty-four-carat *bastard* who seriously needed the help of a good psy-chologist. All he knew was that nothing meant anything to him any more since he'd let Maya go…not even his work. *Including* the play that was currently setting Broadway alight after just two nights.

'Seriously, I could do with a couple of drinks, and I don't want to drink alone tonight. You're about the only one I know who'll talk straight to me and isn't after something… I make no apology for my cynicism, but I do ask your forgiveness for any unkind remarks I may have made earlier. I was actually quite pleased when you rang me to say you were coming over here for a short visit to see how the play was doing. Can you forgive me for my previous bad manners?'

'Sure I can. Lucky for you I was born with such a sweet nature.' Latching onto his arm, Jane reached up on her four-inch stiletto heels and planted a noisy smacker on his cheek. 'Plus I never could resist a handsome well-spoken man when he grovels so nicely!'

'I'm not grovelling, so don't get too carried away. I still only tolerate you because you're my agent.'

'Yeah, and next week they're crowning me the Queen of England!'

'No, no, no, Maya, *querida*! Let me get that. You mustn't lift heavy things now, remember?'

Straightening up from the box of crockery she'd just been about to lift onto the granite worktop of her new flat's kitchen, Maya glanced at her helpful friend Diego with a mixture of exasperation and gratitude. Sturdily built, with the shoulders of a flanker in a rugby team, the Spaniard had practically single-handedly packed and moved the contents of her old studio flat to her new two-bedroom abode down the road in Kensal Rise.

Never mind his usually macho sensibilities—he'd been like the proverbial mother hen round Maya ever since she'd confided to him that she was pregnant. Although not before he'd furiously vowed to 'rough up' the ne'er do well who had thoughtlessly got her in the family way, leaving her to face the prospect of motherhood on her own. When he'd told her that his aunt had a house in Kensal Rise that she rented out, and that the ground-floor flat had recently become vacant, Maya had increased her working hours for the temp agency to meet the new rent, and had even been putting a little by towards the day when she would have to give up her job completely to take care of her baby.

'I'm not going to harm myself if I lift a few light boxes, Diego!' she chided her friend, wincing as he deposited the full-to-the-brim cardboard box onto the counter with a little too much gusto and she heard something inside rattle alarmingly. 'I'm only eight weeks pregnant, and I don't even show yet.'

The Spaniard's dark brown eyes visibly softened as they moved down to Maya's still flat belly beneath her loose white shirt and faded jeans.

'Yet the fact is that you are growing a little one inside you who needs you to be careful and not take unnecessary risks that could harm him or his mother.'

'You know what, Diego?' Her lips tugging upwards in an affectionate smile, exasperation forgotten, Maya touched her palm gently to his roughened cheek. 'One of these days, when you meet the right woman, you're going to be the best father in the whole wide world.'

'And if my wife is as good and beautiful as you, Maya, I will be the happiest man in the whole wide world too!' His pleased grin was quickly followed by a concerned frown. 'Does that crazy, irresponsible man of yours even know what he has done? What he has so foolishly given up?'

Maya flinched, her heart and stomach turning over at the thought of Blaise—at her profound longing to see him again, and at the dreadful hurt and sense of rejection she'd experienced when she'd had to walk away from him in Northumberland and go home. Acute apprehension also deluged her at the prospect of telling him she was pregnant with his child. She'd read in the papers that for the past few weeks he'd been in New York, overseeing the London play that had transferred there. But sooner or later he would be home again, and Maya would have to tell him her news.

After the initial great shock of discovering her condition, she'd been consumed with instant love and strong feelings of protection towards her unborn infant. In her eyes it was an utter miracle, and she felt truly blessed. Even though it wasn't the future she'd dreamed of...to raise a child alone. But how would

Blaise react to the news? *Would he be angry or deadly calm?* Would he reject the reality of her pregnancy completely and deny all responsibility? Or would he want to take charge and calmly make arrangements for the baby's future like some distant, remote stranger, displaying no love or concern for the child's welfare whatsoever?

'He—he's not a man that finds commitment easy, Diego. I think something must have happened when he was young to make him fear it somehow, but he won't discuss it. I told you that. And, to be fair, I guessed that even before I—before we—' She blushed hotly. 'It's unfortunate, but I'm sure when he hears the news he'll want to do the right thing all the same.'

'And if he does not,' Diego growled crossly, folding his arms across his ample chest in his treasured FC Barcelona T-shirt, 'as God is my witness he will have to answer to me!'

Hawk's Lair, Northumberland

His eyes glued to the details of the art auction, and the brief words about it at the beginning of the newspaper article, Blaise sucked in a deep breath, heavily blowing it out again as he tried to get his head round what he'd just read.

'Would you like some more coffee, my dear?' Lottie was hovering beside him, keeping one eye on the sizzling pan of bacon and eggs she was cooking for his breakfast on the stove as well as stealing a curious glance over his shoulder at what he was reading.

'Yes… I mean no, thanks. I've got to go and make a phone call. Excuse me.'

'What about your breakfast?' the housekeeper exclaimed, her voice dismayed as Blaise shot out of his chair and strode to the door.

'Sorry, Lottie… I've got far more important things to think about this morning. Give it to Tom. I'm sure he'd welcome a second breakfast!'

CHAPTER TWELVE

WHEN the phone call came to an end Maya had to sit down, because her legs were shaking so much. She'd scribbled something down on the notepad she now gripped between her hands like a life-raft, and, staring down at what she'd written, she felt a hundred differing emotions storm through her like a cyclone. There was a burning sensation behind the backs of her eyelids, and suddenly tears were sliding and slipping down her cheeks in a hot stream. Not troubling to wipe them away, she slowly moved her head from side to side, as regret and a sadness almost too hard to bear welled up inside her.

'It's time to say goodbye,' she whispered brokenly, 'but I promise I'll never forget you.'

A minute later she got up, put on her trench-coat because outside it had started to rain, locked the door, and then walked rapidly down the street towards the bus stop to catch a bus that would drop her off near Diego's place.

Today was the beginning of a whole new life for her after what she'd just heard, and she needed to share her hopes and fears for the future with a friend…a *good* friend.

It was late in the afternoon by the time Maya got to Camden. The sky had darkened early because of the storm clouds that had gathered overhead, and most of the shoppers were heading homewards. Diego's distinct, brightly painted coffee bar, with its blue-and-white neon sign flickering in the window, was almost empty. The man himself was behind the counter, avidly scanning the sports page in a newspaper, while his young assistant Maria was busy wiping down tables. He glanced up in delight when he heard the bell over the door jangle and saw who it was.

'Maya, *querida*! How are you today?' Moving round the counter with all the grace of a much slimmer man, he enveloped her in a fierce hug. 'Is everything all right? I am surprised to see you when I know the smell of coffee makes you queasy in your condition.'

'I couldn't let a small thing like that stop me visiting you.' Maya smiled, then realised Diego was examining her a little too closely, concernedly shaking his head. 'You have been crying, *querida*…what has happened? Sit down and tell me everything.'

Her friend ordered Maria to bring her a banana milkshake—for the baby!—and they sat opposite each other at a newly cleaned table, under the eye-catching poster of a flamenco dancer dressed in sultry red and black decorating the wall behind them.

Having only just begun her story, Maya glanced round at the sound of the bell jangling above the door and sucked in a shocked breath. *It was Blaise.* She blinked hard to make sure she wasn't dreaming, but she'd know that flawless azure gaze, the carved jaw and the chin with the sexy little crease down the centre anywhere. Her insides mimicked the same intense flamenco as the dancer in the poster.

'What are you doing here?' she asked, and her mouth felt dry as a sun-baked beach at the height of summer. 'I thought you were in New York?'

'I came to find you,' he replied hoarsely, for long moments just standing still and surveying her. Maya knew her gaze must match his for sheer hunger as she stared back at him. He looked every inch the successful Broadway playwright, dressed in a stylish mackintosh, the gold in his hair glistening with damp from the rain.

'I went to your old place and a neighbour told me you'd moved. She wouldn't give me your new address, but she told me that a friend of yours owned this coffee bar and would probably give you a message for me.'

'This is Diego,' Maya murmured, her glance shifting away from his for the briefest second towards the older man sitting opposite her. 'This is his place.'

'Pleased to meet you.' Moving towards their table, Blaise stuck out his hand.

The Spaniard made no move to take it. Instead he abruptly pushed himself to his feet, his expression definitely suspicious. 'And you are…?'

'Blaise Walker.'

'So you are the man that—'

'It's all right, Diego.' With a pleading look Maya managed to still what he had been going to say next. 'I'm sure Blaise isn't staying long…are you?'

'I wouldn't be too sure about that. I need to talk to you, Maya…however long it takes.'

'I need to talk to you too. So maybe—maybe we should go back to my place? We can get a bus just down the road…'

'My car's parked round the corner.'

Feeling queasy, as well as apprehensive, Maya got slowly to her feet. With trembling fingers she attempted to refasten the buttons on her coat, but quickly gave up and left it open. Whatever she and Blaise had to say to each other, it wasn't a conversation to be aired in public. Yet her stomach was fluttering wildly with nerves at the mere thought of being alone with him again. Not only that but probably having to say goodbye to him a second painful time after he'd said what he had to say and then left.

'Diego, I'll give you a call later on tonight, okay?'

'Make sure you do,' the Spaniard replied gruffly, now regarding Blaise with not just suspicion but also antagonism in his eyes. 'I am not happy about how you looked when you came in, and I want to hear

what you were going to tell me and make sure everything is okay.'

'It will keep…and I'll be fine. I promise.'

Saying nothing, his expression implacable, Blaise held
the door open for her to precede him out into the rain.

She'd lost a little weight, he saw with a flicker of alarm.
Her cheekbones were more pronounced, the smooth,
perfect skin stretched over them like pale satin, making
her spellbinding emerald eyes seem huge and her lumi-
nous beauty even more incandescent. But so many
feelings, sensations and fears kept hitting him that it was
difficult for Blaise to stay with one train of thought for
long. Ever since he'd let her go the only thought that
had been and still *was* constant was that he missed her.
He missed her so much that it was as if he'd been in-
flicted with some agonising chest wound that wouldn't
heal. He'd called himself all kinds of imbecile for doing
what he'd done, but insults and fury hadn't helped. Not
when there was still the same underlying fear that daily
ate away at his soul—a corrosive terror that almost par-
alysed him and stopped him from doing what his heart
all but begged and pleaded with him to do.

When he'd seen that article about the art auction in
the newspaper it had finally galvanised him into ac-
tion…finally told him it was time to conquer his fears
and make the one decision he needed to make above
all others.

His gaze flicked interestedly round the recently painted living room of Maya's new flat, noting the more comfortable furnishings and furniture and the sense of space that had been so severely lacking in her previous tiny abode.

During the car journey to get here she had haltingly told him about the opportunity that had come up to move to a bigger place—how she had eagerly grasped it with both hands and how Diego had helped her move. Having met the surly Spaniard who owned the coffee bar Maya liked to frequent, Blaise silently owned to feeling quite put out that she was friends with such a man…*a man who had looked at him as if he'd like to punch a fist right in the centre of his gut.* He smirked grimly.

A couple of pretty cards wishing her happiness in her new home graced the magnolia-painted mantelpiece, he noticed, fighting to gain control over the growing feelings of jealousy and possessiveness that poured through him. *Who had sent her the cards? Was she seeing someone?* Sitting quietly on the sofa across the floor from where he stood, her long legs encased in sheer black hosiery and her hands calmly folded in the lap of her deep burgundy skirt, Maya met his glance steadily, with no hint of the strong emotion that currently tormented Blaise.

'What made you sell the portrait?' he heard himself demand, his heart thudding because it wasn't the first thing he wanted to do. Even now he had to wrestle with the almost overwhelming urge to just haul her up from where she sat and kiss her senseless.

Her emerald gaze remained steady. 'You heard about the sale?'

'How could I not? It made the news in most of the papers, I should think.'

'I needed the money.' Her slender shoulders lifted in what looked like a resigned shrug. 'It was as simple as that.'

'You needed the money before, if the place you lived in was any indication!' Blaise couldn't contain the impatience in his voice. 'Why decide to sell it now?'

'Because there's not just myself to think about any more.'

'You're seeing someone else?'

Everything inside him constricted with despair, fury and tension. *Why had he left it so long to contact her after she left? Why? Why? Why?*

'I'm not seeing anyone else.' Sighing, she rose slowly to her feet, her hands linking restlessly together. 'I'm pregnant, Blaise. I'm afraid I made a mistake about it being a safe time.'

'Pregnant?' The word filled his mind like a snow-storm, blotting out all other thoughts.

'That's why I needed to sell the portrait. I'm keeping the baby, whatever you decide to do, and I didn't want him or her brought up in an atmosphere of tension and uncertainty like I was. I wanted to give my baby a better start and a more secure future.'

'You're going to have a baby? *My* baby?' Again the knowledge deluged him, making it almost impossible to think with any clarity. Then came the terrible fear that he couldn't possibly be a proper father to the child— not if there was the remotest chance that he would turn out like his own father. But in the next instant that unhappy thought died away, and Blaise started to feel genuine excitement and joy pulse through his blood-stream. It took two to make a baby, and ideally two to be his parents and take care of him. Whatever happened, he and Maya were in this together.

'There's no doubt that the baby is yours, Blaise.' Her teeth nibbled a little anxiously at her soft lower lip. 'I've been with no one else.'

'I'm not suggesting anything like that.' He frowned. 'Are you okay? Have you seen a doctor?'

'Both me and the baby are doing just fine.'

'But the portrait…it meant everything to you. I can't believe you sold it. It was a little piece of your father, you said.'

'At the end of the day it's just a painting…if a valu-able one. I was shocked to learn just how valuable. But I'll use the money wisely… I'm sure—I'm sure if my dad were alive he'd want me to use it to help take care of his grandchild.'

'Were you going to let me know about the baby?'

A shadow of hurt flickered in her eyes. 'Of course…
But I knew you were in New York with the play, and
that I'd have to wait until you came back to tell you
face to face.'

'How far along are you?'

'Nine weeks.'

Blaise rubbed his hand round the back of his neck,
thinking hard. Impatiently he pulled his tie loose from his
shirt collar so that he could breathe easier. *It wasn't every
day that a man who had been contemplating a decidedly
lonely future learned that he was to become a father, and
it took some sinking in to get used to the idea.* But the more
he contemplated it, the more he sensed a wild exhilaration
and sense of purpose gathering momentum inside him,
instead of fear and apprehension consuming him.

'So…I'm to become a father?'

'Are you angry?'

'Are you serious? How can I be angry when this
must be the most incredible piece of news I've ever
heard?' In front of Maya now, Blaise caught hold of her
worryingly chilled hands and held them, infusing them
with the heat from his own.

'You mean it?'

'Yes, I mean it! Though I understand why you have
your doubts. I'm not proud of the way I behaved, Maya.
The way I so easily let you leave and made no attempt
to stop you or contact you afterwards.'

Saying nothing, she simply listened.

'I would never have expected you to raise the baby on your own,' he continued, his voice hoarse with regret that she might have believed that. 'I would always have supported him—and you.' Lifting those cold, slender hands to his lips, he tenderly kissed each one in turn.

'So what exactly are you telling me, Blaise? That you want joint custody when the time comes?'

'No, that's not what I'm saying at all.'

'Then—'

Letting go of her hands, Blaise urgently encircled Maya's slender waist to impel her hard against him. For a moment his senses were saturated by her warmth and those delicious feminine curves, and the unmatched feeling of holding her in his arms again almost overwhelmed him.

'I was such a fool to let you go...' He dragged the pad of his thumb over her plump lower lip, sensing heat inflame him as he saw it quiver. 'I had my reasons...but in the cold light of day they seemed preposterous when I started to examine them. But before I tell you about that, I need to ask you something.'

'What is it?'

'Will you marry me?'

Her expression was genuinely shocked, as if that was the very *last* thing she'd expected Blaise to ask her. He could only blame himself for that, he mused bitterly.

'But you're not a man who wants commitment.' She was looking distinctly puzzled. 'You adore women but haven't found one yet that you want to spend the rest of your life with. You made it clear that the possibility of us staying together long-term wasn't even on the cards...that we could enjoy a brief affair but nothing more—least of all marriage.'

'I was wrong. I was wrong because I *did* meet someone I wanted to spend the rest of my life with...*you*, Maya. I used to trot out that rubbish because I couldn't get past the fear that if I committed to a woman I would turn out like my father...become bitter and resentful and harm her in some way.'

'Harm her? Why would you believe that?'

'Because that's what my father did to my mother, and I seem to have inherited his propensity to lose my temper.' He dropped his head for a moment, acutely uncomfortable at finally admitting what he'd been most afraid of.

'Everyone has a temper, Blaise. Even the most seemingly docile people... It's normal...human.' Gently, Maya touched her hand to his cheek and made him look at her. 'It doesn't mean that they're going to be violent.'

'My mother said to me once that she prayed I wouldn't turn out like my father. She loved him passionately, but she was afraid of him too. He'd always been hell to live with. Growing up with such a volatile man was a nightmare sometimes. I never forgot what she said to me. Every time I sensed rage in me I'd wonder—was that a sign? Was I going the same way as him? I even started to jeopardise the new play I've been writing because I wasn't fully exploring the lead character's motivation for leaving home. It wasn't just about him trying to make a dream of happiness come true—*his* father was violent too. That's what ultimately drove him away.'

'It must have been very painful for you all these years—not being able to tell anyone how you felt. I've learned that keeping our fears to ourselves is never the answer, Blaise. They just get bigger and bigger if we don't bring them out into the open and see them for what they really are. They're just ideas we get about ourselves because of something that happens. They're not the truth. I thought similarly to you. I thought because my father behaved like he did, and put all his friends before me, that must mean I was unlovable. When Sean deceived me with another woman it confirmed that view. I felt totally rejected and worthless. I thought our whole relationship had been a lie, based on my fantasies about a happy future together. But then I met you, Blaise, and for the first time I *really* and truly fell for someone.'

'Well, let me tell you now, the notion that you must be unlovable is totally ludicrous!'

Fastening his hands either side of her curvaceous hips, Blaise gave her a brief, hungry, hard kiss on the mouth. When he lifted his head again he was beaming.

'You are the most lovable woman I've ever known... that's ultimately why I couldn't resist you. And I'm going to spend the rest of my life showing you that it's true... It was my own stupid fault, but you broke my heart when you left, Maya.' Lightly he swept back a stray ebony strand of hair where it glanced against her cheek. 'I haven't been able to work, eat or sleep since you went. I'm sure everyone in New York thought I was a miserable git!'

'No…' Softly but emphatically the word left Maya's lips. Incredibly, she was regarding him just as Jane had described the way her husband looked at *her*—as if he'd hung the moon.

'You're not morose or violent or any of those dark things, Blaise… You're just a man who's been hurt. That's hardly a crime.'

'Well, I'm certainly no hero—not the one you deserve. But I am a man who loves you very much and can't live without you.'

'I didn't mean to break your heart.' Maya sighed. 'I only wanted to try and help mend it.'

'Marry me,' he said again, dropping a tender kiss at the side of her mouth. 'Marry me and put me out of my misery once and for all.'

She could hardly believe the urgency in his loving demand. It seemed like a dream when Maya had more than half expected him to reject her all over again after he heard about the baby. She was gratified that he had at last told her why he had let her walk away. Not because he didn't want her…but because he was afraid if he properly committed to a relationship he might end up hurting her physically, just like his father had done to his mother. She could understand how having a fear like that must have haunted him.

The weeks without him had been some of the most despairing Maya had ever spent. All she'd been able to do was think about him, remembering with longing how passionately they had made love and aching down to the very marrow in her bones to see him again. *Her yearning had been multiplied when she'd found out she was carrying his child.* Now he had asked her to marry him, and there really *was* only one answer she could give him.

'I love you, Blaise... I'm not a bit afraid that you would ever hurt me *or* our child, and of course I'll marry you.'

'Wait here.'

'Why?'

She watched in vague alarm as he swiftly left the room. Seconds later she heard the front door open. With her heart helplessly knocking against her ribs, Maya waited anxiously for his return. When he came, he was carrying something square, carefully wrapped in brown paper. He placed it into her hands. The rain had dampened his hair again, and she longed to thread her fingers through the thick gold strands and bring his face down to hers for a long, lingering kiss. Stifling the urge, she stared at the package he'd given her.

'Open it. It's for you,' he urged softly. 'Think of it as an early wedding present.'

Carefully tearing some of the paper packaging away,

Maya gasped when she saw what it was…*her portrait*. Confused as well as elated, she caught her lip between her teeth to stop her emotion from overwhelming her. 'You bought the portrait…to give to me?'

'I knew something had happened when I saw it was up for sale. You would never have sold it unless there was some absolutely compelling reason.' Relieving her of the picture, Blaise laid it against the couch and came straight back to her. 'There's only one place where that portrait belongs, and that's with *you*, sweetheart.'

Reaching out, Maya put her hands against his chest, her expression wide-eyed and shocked.

'But you paid a fortune for it, Blaise! So much money that just the thought of it makes my head spin!'

'If I'd spent ten thousand times that amount it wouldn't be as valuable as you are to me, my darling.'

'I don't know what to say… I'm so overwhelmed that I think I'm going to—'

Blaise's lips covered hers, his tongue slipping hotly into her mouth. He pressed her body close into his even as the tears in her eyes spilled over onto her cheeks. Crying and kissing him at the same time, Maya knew her heart was so full she could hardly comprehend so much joy was possible. Her legs went weak as a newborn lamb's as his deepening kiss and hungrily searching hands on her body made her melt and yearn and ache to hold him closer, without the barrier of clothing.

As if reading her mind, he suddenly scooped an arm

behind her back and lifted her up into his arms, his extraordinary eyes hazy with longing, his well-cut lips quirking in a teasing, provocative grin that made Maya dissolve inside even more.

'As much as I love them, and earn my living by them, I think the time for words has definitely passed, don't you? Where's the bedroom, my darling wife-to-be?'

MILLS & BOON

MAY 2010 HARDBACK TITLES

ROMANCE

Virgin on Her Wedding Night	Lynne Graham
Blackwolf's Redemption	Sandra Marton
The Shy Bride	Lucy Monroe
Penniless and Purchased	Julia James
Powerful Boss, Prim Miss Jones	Cathy Williams
Forbidden: The Sheikh's Virgin	Trish Morey
Secretary by Day, Mistress by Night	Maggie Cox
Greek Tycoon, Wayward Wife	Sabrina Philips
The French Aristocrat's Baby	Christina Hollis
Majesty, Mistress...Missing Heir	Caitlin Crews
Beauty and the Reclusive Prince	Raye Morgan
Executive: Expecting Tiny Twins	Barbara Hannay
A Wedding at Leopard Tree Lodge	Liz Fielding
Three Times A Bridesmaid...	Nicola Marsh
The No. 1 Sheriff in Texas	Patricia Thayer
The Cattleman, The Baby and Me	Michelle Douglas
The Surgeon's Miracle	Caroline Anderson
Dr Di Angelo's Baby Bombshell	Janice Lynn

HISTORICAL

The Earl's Runaway Bride	Sarah Mallory
The Wayward Debutante	Sarah Elliott
The Laird's Captive Wife	Joanna Fulford

MEDICAL™

Newborn Needs a Dad	Dianne Drake
His Motherless Little Twins	Dianne Drake
Wedding Bells for the Village Nurse	Abigail Gordon
Her Long-Lost Husband	Josie Metcalfe

0410 Gen Std LP

ROMANCE

Ruthless Magnate, Convenient Wife	Lynne Graham
The Prince's Chambermaid	Sharon Kendrick
The Virgin and His Majesty	Robyn Donald
Innocent Secretary...Accidentally Pregnant	Carol Marinelli
The Girl from Honeysuckle Farm	Jessica Steele
One Dance with the Cowboy	Donna Alward
The Daredevil Tycoon	Barbara McMahon
Hired: Sassy Assistant	Nina Harrington

HISTORICAL

Tall, Dark and Disreputable	Deb Marlowe
The Mistress of Hanover Square	Anne Herries
The Accidental Countess	Michelle Willingham

MEDICAL™

Country Midwife, Christmas Bride	Abigail Gordon
Greek Doctor: One Magical Christmas	Meredith Webber
Her Baby Out of the Blue	Alison Roberts
A Doctor, A Nurse: A Christmas Baby	Amy Andrews
Spanish Doctor, Pregnant Midwife	Anne Fraser
Expecting a Christmas Miracle	Laura Iding

MILLS & BOON

JUNE 2010 HARDBACK TITLES

ROMANCE

Marriage: To Claim His Twins	Penny Jordan
The Royal Baby Revelation	Sharon Kendrick
Under the Spaniard's Lock and Key	Kim Lawrence
Sweet Surrender with the Millionaire	Helen Brooks
The Virgin's Proposition	Anne McAllister
Scandal: His Majesty's Love-Child	Annie West
Bride in a Gilded Cage	Abby Green
Innocent in the Italian's Possession	Janette Kenny
The Master of Highbridge Manor	Susanne James
The Power of the Legendary Greek	Catherine George
Miracle for the Girl Next Door	Rebecca Winters
Mother of the Bride	Caroline Anderson
What's A Housekeeper To Do?	Jennie Adams
Tipping the Waitress with Diamonds	Nina Harrington
Saving Cinderella!	Myrna Mackenzie
Their Newborn Gift	Nikki Logan
The Midwife and the Millionaire	Fiona McArthur
Knight on the Children's Ward	Carol Marinelli

HISTORICAL

Rake Beyond Redemption	Anne O'Brien
A Thoroughly Compromised Lady	Bronwyn Scott
In the Master's Bed	Blythe Gifford

MEDICAL™

From Single Mum to Lady	Judy Campbell
Children's Doctor, Shy Nurse	Molly Evans
Hawaiian Sunset, Dream Proposal	Joanna Neil
Rescued: Mother and Baby	Anne Fraser

0510 Gen Std LP

JUNE 2010 LARGE PRINT TITLES

ROMANCE

The Wealthy Greek's Contract Wife	Penny Jordan
The Innocent's Surrender	Sara Craven
Castellano's Mistress of Revenge	Melanie Milburne
The Italian's One-Night Love-Child	Cathy Williams
Cinderella on His Doorstep	Rebecca Winters
Accidentally Expecting!	Lucy Gordon
Lights, Camera…Kiss the Boss	Nikki Logan
Australian Boss: Diamond Ring	Jennie Adams

HISTORICAL

The Rogue's Disgraced Lady	Carole Mortimer
A Marriageable Miss	Dorothy Elbury
Wicked Rake, Defiant Mistress	Ann Lethbridge

MEDICAL™

Snowbound: Miracle Marriage	Sarah Morgan
Christmas Eve: Doorstep Delivery	Sarah Morgan
Hot-Shot Doc, Christmas Bride	Joanna Neil
Christmas at Rivercut Manor	Gill Sanderson
Falling for the Playboy Millionaire	Kate Hardy
The Surgeon's New-Year Wedding Wish	Laura Iding

millsandboon.co.uk Community

Join Us!

The Community is the perfect place to meet and chat to kindred spirits who love books and reading as much as you do, but it's also the place to:

- **Get the inside scoop from authors about their latest books**
- **Learn how to write a romance book with advice from our editors**
- **Help us to continue publishing the best in women's fiction**
- **Share your thoughts on the books we publish**
- **Befriend other users**

Forums: Interact with each other as well as authors, editors and a whole host of other users worldwide.

Blogs: Every registered community member has their own blog to tell the world what they're up to and what's on their mind.

Book Challenge: We're aiming to read 5,000 books and have joined forces with The Reading Agency in our inaugural Book Challenge.

Profile Page: Showcase yourself and keep a record of your recent community activity.

Social Networking: We've added buttons at the end of every post to share via digg, Facebook, Google, Yahoo, Technorati and de.licio.us.

www.millsandboon.co.uk